PRAISE FOR *A PLANET F*

BY YOSS

"*A Planet for Rent* is the English-language debut of Yoss, one of Cuba's most lauded writers of science fiction... Yoss' smart and entertaining novel tackles themes like prostitution, immigration and political corruption. Ultimately, it serves as an empathetic yet impassioned metaphor for modern-day Cuba, where the struggle for power has complicated every facet of society."

—NPR, Best Books of 2015

"This hilarious and imaginative novel by Cuba's premier science fiction writer gets my vote for most overlooked novel of the year. Yoss's book imagines a world where Earth is run as a tourist destination by capitalist aliens who have little regard for the planet or its inhabitants. *A Planet for Rent* is a perfect SF satire for our era of massive inequality and seemingly unchecked environmental destruction."

—Lincoln Michel, VICE

"In prose that is direct, sarcastic, sexual and often violent, *A Planet for Rent* criticizes Cuban reality in thinly veiled terms. Cuban defectors leave the country not on rafts but on 'unlawful space launches'; prostitutes are 'social workers'; foreigners are 'xenoids'; and Cuba is a 'planet whose inhabitants have stopped believing in the future.' The book is particularly critical of the government-run tourism industry of the '90s, which welcomed and protected tourists—often at the expense of Cubans—and whose legacy can still be felt today."

—*The New York Times*

"Can one Cuban author boldly go where none have gone before and inspire American readers? Heavy metal rocker turned science fiction writer José Miguel Sánchez (known by his pen name, Yoss) believes he can... Science fiction fans... will be interested in the way Yoss addresses important questions about the future: Who are we? What does it matter to be human? And, what is our place in the universe?... Yoss's novel is part of an international literary canon of science fiction classics that makes invisible walls visible by showing everyday readers how inequality segregates people by class, politics or ethnicity."

—NBC News Latino

"The best science-fiction writers are the peripheral prophets of literature—outsiders who persuade us to explore an often uncomfortable vision of the future that shows us not only what might be, but also what should never be allowed to happen, thereby freeing our imaginations from the shackles of our blind rush toward so-called progress. One such prophet lives ninety miles off the coast of Florida, in Havana, and goes by the name of Yoss... Some of the best sci-fi written anywhere since the 1970s... *A Planet for Rent*, like its author, a bandana-wearing, muscly *roquero*, is completely sui generis: riotously funny, scathing, perceptive, and yet also heart-wrenchingly compassionate... Instantly appealing."

—The Nation

"What *1984* did for surveillance, and *Fahrenheit 451* did for censorship, *A Planet for Rent* does for tourism... It's a wildly imaginative book and one that, while set in the future, has plenty of relevance to the present."

—The Bookseller

"Devastating and hilarious and somehow, amidst all those aliens, deeply deeply human."

—Daniel José Older, author of the
Bone Street Rumba series and *Salsa Nocturna*

"A compelling meditation on modern imperialism... A fascinating kaleidoscope of vignettes... A brilliant exploration of our planet's current social and economic inequities... Yoss doesn't disappoint, sling-shotting us around the world and the galaxy... Striking, detailed... Yoss has written a work of science fiction that speaks to fundamental problems humans deal with every day. This is not just a story about alien oppression; it's the story of our own planet's history and a call for change."

—SF Signal, 4.5-Star Review

"Interesting and entertaining... deeply tied to the island nation's politics with a satirical edge."

—io9

"[Yoss's] work is modern, dynamic and yet deep and thoughtful... It's wildly inventive, imaginative fiction, with a real edge to the writing—there is an energy to the prose that is almost tangible and to get all this through a translation is nothing short of remarkable."

—SFBook.com, 5-Star Review

"Cuba has produced an author capable of understanding science fiction by writing it like it's rock and roll. Yoss is a thoughtful author who simply seems to understand his work and science fiction better than many of us."

—Electric Literature

YOSS

SUPER EXTRA GRANDE

Translated from the Spanish by
David Frye

RESTLESS BOOKS
BROOKLYN, NEW YORK

First Restless Books paperback edition June 2016

ISBN 978-1-63206-056-3
Library of Congress Control Number: 2016938767

Cover design by Edel Rodriguez
Set in Garibaldi by Tetragon, London

Printed in the United States of America

1 3 5 7 9 8 6 4 2

Ellison, Stavans, and Hochstein LP
232 3rd Street, Suite A111
Brooklyn, NY 11215

www.restlessbooks.com
publisher@restlessbooks.com

To Vicente Berovides, professor of ecology and evolution.

To Yoyi, muse of the first version of XXXX... G
from back in 1999, in which laketons were still continents,
a version now lost on account of... better leave it there.

To Elizabeth, my real-life Cosita, who inspired me to write
this second and, I hope, truly definitive version.

SUPER EXTRA
GRANDE

"**BOSS SANGAN,** sludge al frente and a la derecha, ten centímetros knee," Narbuk peevishly announces through my ear buds.

His voice reminds me unpleasantly of a screechy old machine in need of a lube job. But that's not the worst of it. Worst is, he seems to go out of his way to mangle the grammar and syntax of the Spanglish language, stubbornly dropping prepositions and mutilating verbs like he's doing a bad impression of a native in a third-rate holoseries.

Regardless, the Laggoru can monitor my progress from a distance, and the radar he's using gives him the overview of the situation that I want.

The spot he's guiding me towards flashes blue on the 3-D virtual map of the tsunami's intestines, which I can see superimposed on the upper-right-hand corner of my helmet's visor. Doesn't look promising to me, but in the lower-left-hand corner I see Narbuk's face, looking like a hypertrophied iguana, insisting, "Boss Sangan, please mira, check. Ves now. Si the damn bracelet of the gobernador's spoiled wife be there, us probablemente leave." For variety's sake, he now starts in on the complaints. "Agua here smell muy strange después del morpheorol y el laxative. Hoy not be buen día for el tsunami bowel cleanse."

You have to prep before you can operate. In this case, to tranquilize the "patient" before I started exploring its innards, we dissolved enough morpheorol in the water to sedate a small city for a whole week.

Good thing morpheorol doesn't really affect humans.

But we never expected it would take almost half a day for the critter to absorb the sedative through its gills. If we'd known, we'd have injected it intravenously.

I feel like reminding Narbuk that I'm the one taking the risk of traveling through the tsunami's intestines while he's lounging around and following my "inner voyage" over remote imaging from out there. Why should he care if this was a good day for giving an eighteen-hundred-meter-long animal an intestinal cleanse?

As if any day would be.

Hey, a guy could turn that into a pretty good joke.

But no point wasting time working it out. In spite of his, let's say, dietary restrictions, Narbuk will always be a Laggoru, and Laggorus just don't get irony.

Not because they don't understand our language well enough. Narbuk isn't the best example here; some of them even speak it better than half the humans in the colonies.

It's just that in their culture, things either are or they aren't, and that's that. No nuances or shades of meaning for them. That's why they have about as much of a sense of humor as a rock does.

Funny thing is, that's exactly what makes them so hilarious to be around. Not that they ever get why the people who hang out with them are always cracking up.

That's why, among other reasons, they're so appreciated in the Galactic Community.

I was really lucky I could hire Narbuk and even luckier I could keep him. Hardly an hour goes by when he doesn't set me rolling with laughter. Besides, I have to admit, he is really sharp. Three years ago he didn't know any more about veterinary biology than I do about classical Cantonese linguistics, but today he's an incredibly productive secretary-assistant.

Quick learner.

Be that as it may, today I'd better warn him to keep it under his hat. There's too much at stake to risk letting him ruin it with his bellyaching. Governor Tarkon must have at least half a dozen of his men eavesdropping on our frequency. The three or four Amphorians that hang around the dry dock might be listening in, too. We're pretty near their area of influence, true enough, but I still think it's kind of suspicious to find them here.

So I warn Narbuk, "Wátcha tu tongue, lagartija. This is an op oscuro."

Then I aim the vacuum hose at the chosen spot, praying that the jewels we've been hunting for all day will turn up here, inside this clump of sludge.

Of course my prudent command to watch his tongue has the opposite effect on Narbuk.

"Op oscuro, Boss Sangan? La criatura es almost two kilometers de larga, central island naval repair dry dock, much many soldados when no hay guerra? Oscuro impossible. What me decir bad? Me doubt el Gobernador Tarkon only now discover tercera esposa very much spoil, no muy smart," he insists. Narbuk is as indelicate, undiplomatic, and tactless as every other member of his species. And just as genetically incapable of taking a hint. "Bien educated, muy smart mujer no drop wedding bracelet cuesta millones de solaria. No drop bracelet al sea, no drop tsunami mouth."

Bingo! The intake of the portable vacuum hose finally dislodges the object in question from the monster's intestinal mucus, and...

Another disappointment. The clot of sludge doesn't contain a platinum wedding bracelet inlaid with Aldebaran topaz but the semi-fossilized skull of some small local fish, which the tsunami no doubt swallowed thousands of years before we humans invented the González drive. Or even the wheel, most likely. These animals are really long lived. In fact, so far we haven't seen any of them die except from accidents. Possibly only the laketons of Brobdingnag are longer lived.

Shit. How much longer am I going to have to slog through the… the shit of this oversized sea worm?

"The tsunami debió haber startled her when it yawned en su cara and ella found herself mirando at its lovely fangs de veinte metros," I say, trying to stand up for Mrs. Tarkon out of sheer racial solidarity. Though I kind of doubt her "carelessness" was just an accident. From the little I know of female psychology, she most likely felt bored and left out while her husband was dealing with a thousand and one emergencies, and she wanted a little attention. "Olvídalo and keep your eyes en la imagen del radar. Ya debiamos haber encontrado the trinket. I'm getting cansado of this business."

Tsunamis have a pretty rapid metabolism for such huge invertebrates. Not even six tons of morpheorol will keep this worm out of action much longer—and I'd really rather be as far away as possible when it wakes up. I don't think it's going to thank me for this trip through its guts, or for the eleven tons of laxative we first gave it. Orally, of course. An enema would have been too much to ask.

"Job es job," Narbuk philosophized. "Que worth es, worth es well. Yo hope que el pago is generous, compensate very mucho dirty trabajo."

"Te voy a dar some 'very mucho dirty trabajo,' you half-bit Kant. Keep your trap cerrada, or la próxima it'll be you down the critter's gullet," I threaten jokingly, then trace a wide arc in front of me with the vacuum hose, the way a soldier from centuries past might have mowed down half a dozen enemies with rapid-fire tracers from his laser blaster.

Someone might say that wasting time playing games during such a serious mission is tempting fate. But the fact is, after six hours of running around inside a digestive tract that fancies itself a labyrinth, and wading sometimes shoulder deep in crap and gastric juice, and getting your hopes up every time you inspect a lump of indeterminate gunk you find stuck to the mucous membrane, anybody would have given up believing in good luck. And would be feeling sick and tired.

What did I say. Same song, second verse: no bracelet.

"Gimme algo de data, assistant," I tell Narbuk, then wait for his reply. "Según the map, diez more minutes, y I should be coming out the back end... Pero if I don't have Mrs. Tarkon's precious platinum bracelet, tengo miedo que I might be better off quedándome in here."

More than my reputation is at stake. The governor's bodyguards didn't look all that friendly. And forget about the Amphorians. Those helmets of theirs make them look like two-legged bulldogs. Methane-breathing gear on a human world? That gives you something to think about.

Offended, Narbuk replies, "Boss Sangan, me sorry but no can do that. You por favor knock self out si necesita, but animal me da very mucho allergy." As always, he's oversensitive to any allusion I make to his peculiar problem. "Me Laggoru banned y no como meat because no hunt. Tú sabes."

The reptilian Laggorus are also famous throughout the Galactic Community for eating nothing but meat they've hunted themselves. And they hunt without energy weapons or projectile guns or gizmos of any sort, using nothing but their terrifying fighting claws. Old-school, straight-up predators.

But of course, just my luck, the assistant I hired is the only vegetarian wacko of the whole lot.

And he doesn't get why I think he's funny.

Sure, could be worse. Narbuk doesn't eat meat, but he's as good as the best of them at handling the retractable steel claws Laggorus use for hunting and fighting. With him by my side, I'm never afraid of a bar brawl.

Not that I've been to many bars lately. But when I do go, there aren't many guys who dare to tangle with me.

I admit, I don't know the first thing about karate-do or judo. Or wushu, baguazhang, pencak silat, krav maga, or any other secret martial art. I hardly even have to resort to my fists.

As Sun Tzu wrote thousands of years ago, the best strategy is not the one that grants victory in battle, it's the one that lets you win without even fighting.

Intimidation, in a word.

And it turns out I'm a born expert in that art.

The good old-fashioned art of fear.

Faced with that, almost any opponent will opt for the equally ancient and effective martial art of turning tail and running.

Hey, don't think I go around threatening people or putting on childish strong-man demonstrations, like smashing stuff or lifting heavy objects with one hand. The truth is, I don't have to do a *thing*.

Let's just say, I'm a little taller and bigger all around than your average human.

In fact, quite a bit taller and heavier than the average *Homo sapiens*.

The honest truth is, very few humans are bigger than me.

So what usually happens with most of the hotheads out itching for a fight is, they take one glance at me, and—after practically falling over backwards trying to look me in the eyes—they whisper something to their buddies and go back to staring down the other big guys at the bar.

They never bother Narbuk, either. Not only because his species has a reputation for being quick and lethal with their claws (they don't keep them for show).

Turns out, while the Laggoru weighs barely half as much as me (these reptilian guys are really slim), he's also four inches taller. A real giant among his kind, as I am among mine.

That was another thing for us to bond over from the beginning.

It's definitely nice to hang with someone who doesn't constantly make you think you're freakishly large by human standards, and who genuinely understands when you complain about the crap that seems to have been made with dwarves in mind.

The hell with statistical ergonomics. We big people have rights, too.

If you disagree, go find yourself a tag-team partner. The Laggoru and I challenge you, here and now. Or wherever, whenever.

Before long, Narbuk and I were inseparable buddies. My mother always told me to hang out with the biggest guy around. Not bad advice, I admit. Just a little hard to do when you yourself are always the biggest guy around.

As if the problem of size weren't enough, there's also the matter of sex...

That's a long, complicated story.

Before the Laggoru came along, I had two other secretary-assistants. Both females.

So the jealous sorts can run their mouths off about my supposed misogyny...

Enti Kmusa, the first assistant I hired, was a human from Olduvaila. A direct descendant of the Maasai people, she was tall and skinny, like most *Homo sapiens* individuals who grow up on low-gravity worlds. Almost as tall as me, in fact. The Maasai were a famously tall ethnic group to begin with.

Slender, elegant, almost feline, especially in the way she walked... That was Enti. I could easily imagine her trekking across her great-great-great-great-great-grandparents' ancestral savannah. I called her "my black panther." And I have to say, exotic as she seemed at first, with her pure black skin, her large, dark eyes, her shaved head, and her filed teeth, she was also incredibly beautiful.

She was also organized and efficient, and she exuded natural likability from every pore. The largest creatures in the galaxy didn't scare her or make her foolishly squeamish. As a result, clients began to swarm my office.

They came from all over, from every race.

But that was where the problems started, too. The lanky, stunning descendant of the Maasai had, let's say, some minor prejudices against the other intelligent species of the Milky Way.

No matter how much energy the Human Section of the Galactic Community Coordinating Committee spends trying to fight racism (now that it's finally been convinced to give up denying there is such a thing), it seems this complex problem will continue to haunt us humans for centuries.

It must be our civilization's fault, with its peculiar and violent history, I guess. Few intelligent species have attained space travel with as many visible racial differences among themselves as we have.

When "my black panther" started losing clients for me through her flagrant xenophobia, I thought about firing her, but after considering her other valuable qualities I decided instead to hire another girl to help with the non-humans...

Nobody can accuse me of being intolerant and intransigent, or of denying people a second chance.

I think I picked a good one, and in fact it all seemed like smooth sailing at first. An-Mhaly was a Cetian, and like almost all Cetians she was nearly as tall as me, but also as pleasant as a professional flight attendant and as delicate as a porcelain doll, with a fascinating smile. As if that weren't enough, her beautiful contralto voice went perfectly with her height.

Like all Cetians, of course, she also had yellow eyes with no visible pupils, skin that went purple or mauve when she got excited, a retractile spiny crest on the top of her head, a three-forked tongue in a toothless mouth that harbored one of the most complex and efficient mastication systems in the galaxy, and six plump mammary glands.

The first time you see a Cetian female, it's impossible not to think of the old joke (dating back to before the González drive, you know) about one guy who asks another guy, "Te gustan your women con lots of tits?" The other guy says, "Not really. Más than three son sort of a turn-off, pa' decirte la truth."

I later learned that, because of a whole bunch of details that a simple human boor like me can't even appreciate, other Cetians consider An to be an extraordinary beauty. But as for me, I wouldn't have cared if she'd won Miss Galactic Community. Long story short, I didn't find her bosomy abundance all that stimulating, erotically speaking. Quite the contrary.

If I'd been a thirsty baby I might have thought differently, of course...

Call me a racist if you must... but the truth is, even though her species is the closest to human of any in the Galactic Community (according to interspecies medical specialists, at least, and they should know, eh?), I've always thought that calling Cetians "humanoids" stretches the meaning of the word too far.

Maybe anthropoid, at most. Or better yet, gynecoid.

Now, I still found her pretty—but only in the same way I might think a purebred horse or a tiger is handsome. Still doesn't mean I'd want to go to bed with them. For the record.

Sure, I must have been swayed by knowing that any attraction I felt for her would be doomed to fail. If her six splendid breasts wowed me (to make matters worse, she always kept them on gloriously open display, Cetian style), if they gave me the harebrained thought I might get intimate with her... No, better not even think about it.

Some hook-ups are, shall we say, just plain physiologically impossible.

Not her fault, I admit. It's just sheer bad luck that her exotic biology is incompatible with ours. But you know, you can't squeeze blood from a turnip.

Or inject a turnip with blood, if you're a donor...

That's where my problems began.

Enti and An-Mhaly could be (and indeed were!) outstanding secretaries and well-disciplined assistants. They were physically strong and didn't gag at the sight of blood, guts, or other disgusting bodily fluids from any species of oversized creature. But regardless. They were still female.

So what happened next was entirely my fault, no one else's.

I should have seen it coming. Women (and by extension, apparently all female humanoids, or gynecoids, in general) are like cats, or like the marbusses of Mizar that all women love so much: When you call them they don't come, and when you don't call them, there's no way to get rid of them.

Professional gigolos are well acquainted with this paradox. They take advantage of it with what they call the "inaction strategy" or "boredom as bait" or something along those lines. And they say it *always* works.

I guess there's some strange part of the female psychology that simply can't stand being ignored by a male, interpreting it as a personal insult or a challenge they have to confront, come what may, whatever it takes.

Even if what it takes is joining forces with someone who might be her worst imaginable enemy under other circumstances.

As a result, what a coincidence! Both assistants fell in love with me (or told me they did) just a few months after they started working together.

I later came to believe it was a conspiracy, something they'd agreed on.

Because each of them declared their love to me within a few hours of the other.

Kind of suspicious, don't you think?

Though I suppose they'd deny it, even if you boiled them alive.

Jan Amos Sangan Dongo, the most eligible bachelor alive, chased by the greatest beauties of two species.

Ha.

Must have been my good heart, I guess. Because if it was my body, forget about it.

I'm well aware that I have the body of a troll. And a face not even a troll would touch.

Me, a Don Juan.

Ha.

That's right. I never tried to kindle any kind of romance with my two assistants—and now I realize that might have been a terrible mistake. I probably should have at least traded a few double entendres with them, commented on how physically attractive they were... I don't know, anything but pretend I didn't find any sexual charm in either of them.

Which, to start with, wasn't even close to true.

In general, my opinion is that love and work don't mix. My parents taught me as much, without even resorting to words.

But I don't want to think about my parents now.

And hey, it's not like I was a saint. A man can't live on bread alone, especially not if he's a veterinarian biologist... as some of my clients can attest. (Cetians apart, of course.)

But the office was the office, and my assistants were my assistants, nothing more.

Human or Cetian, no discrimination.

My policy: Don't shit in the dining room.

So, since I wasn't interested in having either of them as a partner (or to be honest, since I didn't think it was in the cards—I maybe could have had a crazy one-night stand with Enti Kmusa, but I'd have been crazy to even think about it with An-Mhaly), and since, in spite of all their feminine solidarity, the two "hopelessly in love" females were starting to act jealous of each other, especially around me, I decided to make a clean break and simply get rid of them both. No explanations. A triangle is a pretty precarious geometrical figure.

Naturally, I had to give them each a hefty severance package for firing them without notice. Plus, for the Cetian—this is one of the downsides of the Galactic Community Coordinating Committee and its painstakingly achieved interracial equality!—a substantial bonus for "xenophobic discrimination" and "psychological distress."

I guess it wasn't all that much. Poor kid even tried taking her own life after I rejected her.

I felt terribly guilty for several days, until I found out it's a fairly common practice among her race. In some ways the Cetians remind me of the samurai from ancient Japan on Earth: they often prefer death to dishonor.

Aha! Okay, then. Learning that fact made me feel a little better.

Only a tiny bit better, though, to tell the truth.

The whole business, with all the subsequent complications over the Cetian, left me so paranoid about the idea of "assistants" (female or not, because in this era of galactic sexual liberation and interspecies pansexuality, you never know) that I worked solo for the next few months. And in my field, working without a good assistant isn't hard, it's impossible.

The worst of it was that, going overnight from two assistants to none, my productivity took a nosedive. My client list, too. Robots can help a little in certain situations, of course, but nothing takes the place of a capable assistant with gumption. Especially not a secretary-assistant, and a fairly bright one, like Enti or An-Mhaly.

Even less both of them at once.

That's how things were going for me when the Laggoru, Narbuk-Alr-Quamal-Tahlir-Norgai, contacted me over the holo-net one day.

He rubbed me the wrong way right from the start with his clumsy mangling of Spanglish. And when he admitted to having no experience as a secretary or a lab assistant, not to mention the "minor detail" that, even though he's a Laggoru, he's pretty uncomfortable around animals in general (a generous description of his strange zoophobia), I was tempted to tell him then and there, "Gracias, but don't call me, mejor yo te llamo, y don't hold your breath."

But no other candidates tried out for the job, he needed it urgently, and I was just as desperate to find an assistant who, even if he wasn't a model of efficiency, at least wouldn't start making uncomfortable erotic passes at me...

These are strange times. One of the downsides of galactic integration is that some intelligent races have practically turned interspecies sex into a sport. Kerkants, for example. They can hardly create a family anymore without "cohabiting" with at least two different rational species first. No matter what sort of air they breathe.

But Laggorus, being traditionalists, still strongly disapprove of such promiscuity.

Must be because they have six or eight sexes (it still isn't completely clear), none of which corresponds directly to the male or female of humans or any other species. Some believe that not even the Laggorus themselves fully understand their baroque system of sexual castes and sub-castes. Wouldn't surprise me.

I didn't care exactly which sex Narbuk belonged to. Just so long as he was equally uninterested in my sex.

Be that as it may, Narbuk-Alr-Quamal-Tahlir-Norgai came for an interview with his future employer with little hope of getting the job... But the fact is, whether because I needed an assistant so badly, or because he was even taller than I am, or because he immediately admitted to being misogynistic and heterosexual, he started work for me that same day.

It was a good move. Though even now I'm not totally sure he's exactly what we'd call a male if he were human, I'm quite certain he has absolutely no sexual interest in me.

Of course, one month later my formerly well-ordered professional schedule was in total chaos. Besides having no sense of humor, Laggorus have no talent whatsoever for office work.

Though, to tell the truth, I can't complain. I don't know how, but I've almost doubled my old client list...

Maybe orderliness is overrated after all.

"Boss Sangan, sludge, dos metros, front." His screaking voice shakes me from my reflections.

I notice his dorsal pleats slowly distending.

What does that mean? Interpreting the emotions of a creature who doesn't express his feelings through facial muscles is kind of complicated. Exhaustion? Or hope, maybe?

"Algo ring-shape inside. Me know us find already muchos fish bones. Now el corazón tell me something mucho good," he declares.

Ah, it seems there is hope, then. I sip some water through my helmet's built-in tube and slog through the mud (not actually mud, unfortunately) like a hippo in my excited rush to the spot he's marked on the map.

You have to take a Laggoru seriously when he tells you his heart tells him something. After all, Laggorus have six hearts, not one. They also give birth to live young instead of laying eggs. Of course, they aren't really reptiles. Most of the zoological categories we apply to fauna on Earth have no meaning in any other ecology in the galaxy. Our planet is not the measure of all things.

Just in case, I prepare myself for another disappointment, in the best Zen way.

"Seek y encuentra, hunt and captura. That's what la vida is all about. Has it occurred alguna vez to you, mi esteemed colega Narbuk-Alr-Quamal-Tahlir-Norgai, that when tú vas hunting por algo o looking por alguien, you have todo tipo of disappointments, you take lots of decisiones equivocadas—but el verdadero joy of discovery solamente comes once? The hunt is therefore más importante than the result."

After a short silence, the Laggoru quickly retracts his dorsal pleats, which I believe is a clear display of disapproving surprise, and replies, "No, Boss Sangan. Never me think esto. Sound estúpido. If hunt es más importante, why hunt algo? Maybe find it. Mejor hunt nothing, then never find nada, verdad?"

"Huh. Yo guess so," I mumble, cursing his implacable logic as I point the vacuum hose towards the latest piece of sludge and pray to all the gods I don't believe in, the gods of Earth and every other planet, that this will finally be Mrs. Tarkon's damn wedding bracelet, not another sludge-covered fish vertebra.

I'm dying to get out of here...

If it's the trinket, and her loving spouse keeps his promise, I'll be a little richer than I was before.

Well, a lot richer, actually.

And why wouldn't Mr. Tarkon do what he promised? You might think an ordinary veterinarian biologist wouldn't pay attention to these things, but in lots of human colonial enclaves the governor is practically a god. The Amphorians hang around him for a reason: There are trade deals with Nerea only he can authorize.

Contraband deals, too...

Hmm, that's an interesting thought. It might explain a lot... Is there any illegal substance trafficking or alien bribery going on around here? Wouldn't shock me. Tarkon seems to have quite a budget at his disposal. Not unlimited, but pretty flexible at least. Locating me and getting me here from the other side of the galaxy in less than two hours couldn't have been exactly cheap. A round trip in a private ship equipped with a González drive, a shuttle flight to the planet's surface—fast, I don't deny it, but I had to put up with eight brutal *g*'s for a few *loooong* minutes.

The orbital space elevator would have been more comfortable, but slower. And cheaper, too, plenty cheaper.

Not even counting details like the cost of a few tons of sedatives and laxatives, or the emergency bonus, my fees aren't exactly modest.

They couldn't be. Unusual expertise is expensive, and I'm unique.

The sign on my office door on Gea and my holonet ads all say the same thing: NOTHING IS TOO BIG FOR US.

As long as it's alive...

I'm Dr. Jan Sangan, the "Veterinarian to the Giants." The only veterinarian biologist or animal doctor in the whole galaxy, human or alien, who specializes in extremely large organisms.

Tsunamis clearly come under my purview. These little cuties, the symbols of Nerea, are the largest known aquatic life form in the galaxy. So far, at least.

Of course, there are much larger free-floating organisms in space. Genuine leviathans of weightlessness, such as the ten-kilometer-long threshers. And concholants, which can be up to twice that size. Not to mention the laketons of Brobdingnag, planetary leviathans that make even those titans of weightless space look tiny.

But, regardless, tsunamis are *huge*. Males of up to three kilometers long have been found. They owe their expressive name to the fact that when they swim rapidly or whip their tails in anger or in play, they make waves reminiscent of the waves caused by seaquakes on Earth.

Nerea, their home planet, is a giant ocean dotted with three or four archipelagos. The water is fifty kilometers deep in some parts. Good thing, too, because tsunamis would find even the Marianas Trench in the Pacific a tight squeeze.

Though tsunamis, like many living species in the galaxy, have no exact equivalent in the taxonomy of pre-González drive Earth zoology, they could be placed halfway between echinoderms and polychaete annelids.

That explanation should satisfy all the laymen, I'm sure.

You could also think of them as gigantic sea worms. Basically, they're huge worms with segmented bodies covered in bony plates (articulated exoskeletons), legless, with multiple hearts (two per segment; as for Laggorus, heart attacks don't cause these critters much more than mild discomfort), and so on and so forth. They are hermaphrodites and reproduce simply, without going through metamorphosis; females of reproductive age lay eggs that hatch into small versions of adult tsunamis.

Too large to be bothered by predators, tsunamis swim wherever they please, and when they're hungry they simply open their cavernous circular mouths, filtering entire cubic kilometers of water through the sieve formed by their enormous teeth (their only function), then swallow everything trapped in the net. They are the Nerean equivalent of Earth's blue whales, though they often swallow "planktonic" organisms half the size of a full-grown man.

At first, the new human colonizers on the planet were appalled by the amount of edible biomass these coldblooded behemoths were consuming and feared they would damage their fishing boats and ferries, so they tried to exterminate them with bombs, mines, and torpedoes.

But their exoskeletons proved so tough and their tissues regenerated so quickly and with such vitality that the colonizers soon realized it would take too many powerful bombs to destroy them all. The shockwaves alone would have destroyed much of the rest of the planet's rich marine life, too.

Their next plan was to poison them, or engineer viral plagues specifically targeting tsunamis. Of course the Ecology Subcommittee of the Galactic Community would never have allowed anything so risky, biologically speaking. Also, luckily, someone realized in time that leaving thousands of tsunami corpses to decompose all at once would create a terrible hygiene problem. There simply aren't enough scavenger organisms in the Nerean ecosystem to process that many enormous corpses at once. The risk of epizootic disease would be too great.

Taking all of this into consideration, plus the "friendliness" that made them tourist attractions (many visitors pay good money to experience the thrill of swimming with these titans — while wearing ultraprotective suits, of course; the "frolicsome" creatures never attack anything too big to swallow, and we humans are a little large for them, but you might as well guard against a chance swipe of the tail that could almost send you into orbit, right?), not to mention their status as the planet's unique and iconic species, the human colonizers finally decided to let the tsunamis continue happily scarfing down most of the seafood on their planet.

I imagine they also came to understand that any cure would be worse than the illness. As is so often the case in ecology.

That's what I call taking lemons and making lemonade.

Though many people still get a shock every time one of these "harmless little worms" pokes its enormous cylindro-conical head through the water's surface.

I can perfectly picture Mrs. Tarkon, leaning sensually against the rail of the high-speed ferry on which local political bosses transport her powerful husband from one island to another, playing with the limpid water... when suddenly one of those gigantic maws emerges beside her, the innocent tsunami version of a kid jumping out from behind a column and shouting, "Boo!"

Or rather, in this case, "BOOOOOO!"

Maybe I misjudged her; you can't blame her for dropping the bracelet. It's a miracle she kept the hair on her head...

"How go todo, Boss Sangan?" Narbuk asks, worried by my silence. "Be problemas? Malos intestinal parasites? It be jewel o no?"

My assistant isn't kidding about the parasites. The "illegal aliens" these super-extra-grande creatures may harbor often constitute the greatest danger to those who venture inside them.

Once when I was working inside a juggernaut, removing an *in situ* pulmonary neoplasm, half a dozen freeloading nematodes almost half a meter long decided I was a competitor and, more than willing to get rid of their bothersome rival, attacked me with their suckers.

Their circular mouths produced a powerful acid. Good thing I was wearing my ultraprotective suit, which they weren't able to pierce. But it was an experience I'm not anxious to go through again. Not one bit.

Fortunately I haven't found any unexpected guests inside the tsunami. If juggernauts—mollusks from the planet Colossa that are "only" six hundred meters across—can host acid-spewing worms like those, this giant could be infested with parasites twice the size of a rhinoceros on Earth.

"No. If there had been alguna, the laxative must have gotten rid de ella. As for the sludge—todavía I can't say," I grumble, disappointed. "It's resisting, por ahora. Must be a very old cyst. Dáme more time."

Indeed, the mass adhering to the mucous membrane of the anesthetized giant's intestine won't budge, unmoved by the suction hose.

I turn up the power and keep going, absorbed in thought.

Such a fuss over a simple bracelet. If it had been a wristband terminal belonging to any citizen of Nerea, it would have been tough luck, adiós, fuggedaboutit. After all, it's so cheap to make them, so easy to buy a new one.

But this was the governor's respectable wife's very own priceless, irreplaceable platinum wedding band, inlaid with Aldebaran topaz, so of course it was a disaster.

Tarkon's security detail reacted swiftly. One of the muscular bodyguards grabbed a harpoon gun (there's one on board every ship on Nerea) and tagged the monster with a radio transmitter dart—showing off his excellent aim in the process, since it's never a bad idea to angle for a personal recommendation for your next job from an influential governor.

Then they dumped hundreds of gallons of fish blood (the best possible bait) into the water to draw the tagged giant into a shallow naval repair dock nearby. Shallow for a tsunami, that is; it's more than two hundred meters deep. They penned it in there by lowering the sluices and brought me in as quickly as possible.

Good thing the lovely little beastie didn't start wagging its tail before I got here. No matter how strong the monomolecular steel a sluice gate is made from, it could not withstand more than a few blows from an armored tail half a kilometer long and weighing dozens of tons.

Setting a new galactic speed record, I was here just four hours after the worm swallowed the bracelet uninvited. Since the metal detector found no trace of the jewel at the bottom of the dry dock, I deduced that it must still be inside the worm's guts.

Wasting no time, Narbuk and I anesthetized it by filling the dock with morpheorol. Using a couple of cranes, we lifted its head above the waterline, and just when it looked like the whole operation was going to be easy as pie—localize the bracelet, give the worm a little jab, and extract it...

Things started getting complicated.

Tsunamis are blind as bats. Their most important sense organ for detecting prey in the oceans of Nerea is electromagnetic.

If anybody plans to press a metal detector against the skin of an animal that can sense electromagnetic fluctuations of a few microvolts or a tenth of a gauss ever again, he'd better warn me first—so that I can get as far away as possible.

Half a galaxy away would be nice.

For the record, it wasn't my idea. A certain irresponsible Laggoru came up with it... But in any case, the immediate result of the attempt was a reflexive flick of the tsunami's tail that sent a couple dozen tons of water sailing into the air. The water fell more or less uniformly onto Mr. Tarkon, his wife, their bodyguards, the local political honchos and their guards, the Amphorians... and me.

Most ironic of all, the only person that the downpour missed was Narbuk himself. Thanks to his animal allergy, he was standing a good hundred meters back.

Since the "find and recover" tack was obviously not going to work, I went to plan B: force the worm to let go of it. The massive dose of laxatives that we administered orally worked great. In less than five minutes, the stuff filling the dock wasn't exactly water anymore... and the smell forced us all to put on gas masks.

You could tell right away, our tsunami lives on a fish-based diet.

And its stomach is so big that a good part of the menu must have time to rot inside before it even starts getting digested.

A lovely scent for aiding digestion, to be sure.

Everyone whose appetite is piqued by scatology, raise your hands... Sorry if I didn't raise mine. I had one hand busy pinching my nose and the other covering my mouth to keep me from retching.

Without much luck, I admit.

Good thing we didn't give it the laxative before trying the metal detector, otherwise we would have gotten splashed with... Better not even think about it.

But the damn bracelet still refused to appear.

When my stomach was more or less back to normal, it occurred to me that the priceless jewel might have gotten caught in one of the creature's stomach pleats, or lodged in one of its intestinal folds, and I decided to go after it the old-fashioned way.

In situ.

Even if we had something that could overcome the minor obstacle of its exoskeletal plates, it would have been insane to try drilling through the epidermis of a creature with a nervous system so rudimentary that even while deeply sedated it was capable of reflexive movements such as the unforgettable crowd-bathing swipe of the tail. Nobody wanted to risk a second shower, especially since this time the water falling on us wouldn't precisely be crystalline.

So with a vacuum hose in my hand, and wearing a proper anti-magnetic, everything-proof suit that an aide to Mr. Tarkon had quickly commandeered from one of the planetary system's solar patrol ships (I'd have been crazy to go in without one, after the incident with the little worms and their acid suckers inside the juggernaut), I marched smugly, a new and voluntary Jonah, straight up to the monster's jaws.

My thinking was that, if animals half the size of a man fit through its mouth, I could get inside, too. With a little effort, some lubricant, and a bit of pushing, of course.

Twenty minutes later, perhaps due to my somewhat larger-than-average body type, it was proving to take an awful lot of pushing. Not only by me, but also by four of Tarkon's bodyguards, who were trying to use brute muscular strength (something they don't lack, let me point out) to shove me down the monster's gullet.

Since none of my lubricants were helping much either, I cut to the chase and injected twenty kilos of an extra-powerful muscle relaxant straight into the worm's pharynx. This dilated the creature's throat enough to let me through, making me the first veterinarian biologist to study the digestive system of the largest aquatic animal in the galaxy from the inside—and while the animal was still alive.

That was six hours ago.

Since then I've been wading ponderously in my ultraprotective suit (designed to protect an astronaut from cosmic rays and micrometeorite impacts in the weightlessness of space, it isn't exactly light or easy to move in on the planet's surface, not even with the aid of its powerful servomotors), through a thick, dark haze that my helmet's headlamp can't truly dissipate.

Luckily, after my tight squeeze down the tsunami's throat, its esophagus and stomach both turned out to be large enough to walk through standing upright, which was really something for me. I could even have parked a small spaceship inside if I'd had one handy.

The cartridges of monster muscle relaxants I brought with me have allowed me to make my way through the valves of the digestive system, from one to the next: stomach, small intestine, and finally, large intestine. I still have two shots, which I'm saving for my triumphal exit: the anal sphincter.

Lucky I can't smell the liquid I'm walking through. Sometimes up to my waist, sometimes all the way up to my neck. Glad I'm not a Juhungan now. With no sense of sight or sound, they rely entirely on smell, touch, and taste to understand the world. This would not be any fun for them, I'm sure.

Ever since the laxative episode, I thought the whole operation stank, no pun intended. But I never expected I'd be regressing to my infancy. Playing with poo—and for keeps, on a grand scale.

I don't even want to think what would happen if the ultraprotective suit failed...

It'd make for a pretty tragicomic epitaph: ASPHYXIATED IN EXCREMENT.

Of course, there's shit and then there's *shit*.

The laxative was a good idea... Considering the consistency of the fecal matter the colossus expelled in its first bowel movement, I would have needed a sonic drill or an even more powerful excavation tool to make my way through a full colon.

Maybe the critter had been constipated, and that's why it had surfaced, to swallow some air...

This piece of sludge here won't come loose. With all the accretions removed, it turns out to be a nearly perfect sphere, some ten centimeters in diameter. In the dim light of my personal spotlights it looks an iridescent white, like mother-of-pearl.

A fecal pearl? Interesting... But now's not the time to study digestive-system oddities.

I'm starting to lose my patience. Narbuk, who can see everything from his vantage point, tells me it's less than a hundred meters to the back end. But I'd rather buy Mrs. Tarkon a new bracelet, Aldebaran topaz-encrusted platinum and all, than go through the whole business of sedating this monumental worm and inspecting its digestive system a second time...

So I give the old sphere a few light taps with my ceramic-armored glove, testing it...

Hurray for intuition! On the third tap it splits in half, proving to be more a thin crust than a gelatinous coating.

And, hallelujah, the glimmering bracelet falls straight into my hand!

Almost clean even.

Almost. Let's not exaggerate.

A moment of triumph like this makes the whole intestinal trek of the past few hours seem worth it.

I dance a quick jig, shit-kicking included.

"Misión accomplished—got it," I announce, terse but contented, unceremoniously pocketing the bauble in a flap of the suit. I keep moving along, much more quickly now. "I'm heading out de aquí like a rocket, Narbuk. Quieres saber something funny? Sabes what pearls are? The bracelet was encased in a structure muy similar. Fecal pearls! Probablemente tsunamis secrete a kind of nacre, aunque they aren't mollusks, to proteger themselves from contaminantes de heavy metal. Platinum es básicamente inert, though... They must grow increíblemente quickly también, unlike oyster pearls en la Earth. I wonder if they'd be worth algo..."

"Boss Sangan," Narbuk cuts me off. "Me know you gran científico, but better olvidar las pearls and theories por ahora. Tsunami wake soon. Heart beat más rápido, me detect primer nerve impulses."

Shit.

Would it be too scatological to say that things are looking dark brown?

Not at all. Literally, shit... And here I am in it up to my chest, that's the worst part.

"I'm... casi... out," I say to calm him, panting as I try to break the galactic speed record for sprinting in an ultraprotective suit through a colon filled with mysterious liquids. "But... just en caso... get ready... para sedar it again..."

"Yo very sorry, Boss Sangan." With his characteristic sense of timing, the Laggoru pours the proverbial bucket of cold water on my idea. "Me already think esto. Tarkon aides dicen que you use all Nerea morpheorol, primera dosis. También say Amphorians have colony near. Only dos días para produce other ton, they will."

Great. Wonderful news. It never rains, it pours. So there won't be any more sedatives coming? Not for... another two days? Nobody bothered to tell me that little detail. Probably because they guessed (and rightly so) that if I'd known there wasn't enough morpheorol for a second dose, I never would have gone so happily into the guts of the tsunami.

I suddenly remember a character out of Cuban folklore, whom my mother always told me about... *Chacumbele, que él mismito se mató*. Chacumbele, who killed himself, all by himself.

But what can I do now?

"Hold on to the brush, porque I'm taking the ladder," one housepainter said to the other.

Nothing to do but to run faster.

"Oh... magnífico," I joke, panting. "So... in just dos días... Tarkon y estos guys... can sleep bien... after mi funeral."

"Boss Sangan kind man, worry por los demás. But morpheorol be not bueno for humanos," says Narbuk, completely serious. "Por favor, now hurry. Peristaltic contractions, esophagus. Colon, un minuto. Me think este es dangerous sign..."

"Piss off, Narbuk," I grumble, knowing perfectly well what it's a dangerous sign of.

Luckily I can see the great, wrinkled dark star of the beast's anal sphincter. I don't think I ever thought an ass looked so beautiful. Of course, I'd never seen such a big one before... And never from the inside.

"See that, tú pesimista Laggoru? Yo estoy at the back door; ahora I'll just inject the muscle relaxants, y..."

And of course, I run out of time.

With an impressive rumble that the microphones in my helmet amplify even more, *something* huge slams into me from the back. My instinctive reaction is to hold on to the mucous membrane of the tsunami's colon with all the power of the servo-motors in my gloves—and doing this saves me: By the time the force of the tremendous semiliquid flatulence washes me away, the anus has relaxed enough that I emerge without losing any limbs in the violent process.

Though it hasn't been a dignified exit by any means, but rather an outright expulsion.

Along with thousands of liters of mushy organic residue, I fly nearly thirty meters, then fall into the muck filling the naval dry dock. I plummet straight to the bottom, burdened by the leaden weight of my ultraprotective suit.

From down here I watch the tsunami, now conscious again, rising with the majesty of an offended sea deity and swimming nimbly and capably away.

Then the governor's men rescue me. And I surface with the bracelet in my hand, so that they can all witness my success.

But as soon as I emerge, everyone wrinkles their noses, several of them barely succeed in suppressing their gag reflexes... and Mrs. Tarkon, who has impetuously come running over, anxious, I guess, to put on her beloved bracelet, vomits uncontrollably on the spot.

"Perdón, Boss Sangan," Narbuk tells me from afar, "pero you smell mucho bad."

"Narbuk, if eighteen hundred metros of sea leviathan had expelled you de su colon con un..." I begin, but I quickly realize there's no point in making excuses for myself. This isn't the best time to be so... pedantic. There'd be no point, and if I turned it into a joke, the pun itself would stink. "Go on, olvídate about it, solamente demand they give us a biological decontamination tent *ahora*. I don't even quiero to find out qué this suit smells like en el outside. Supongo que they'll incinerate it instead of putting it back. Oh, y cuando you ask Gobernador Tarkon to pay us, try de convencerlo he should add algo extra for... what do you piensas, does 'hazards to psychological health' suena good?"

*

If I ever sit down to write my autobiography, it'll probably start like this:

I was born on a Second Wave colonial world with an unusual origin story. The first settlers there were three thousand descendants of Cubans who left Earth in four homemade spaceships, trying to enter Yumania illegally... But they got lost along the way. They named the place where they landed Coaybay, which in the language of their distant Taíno ancestors meant something like Paradise.

Then I might go on:

I'm an only child, an uncommon status in this era of galactic expansion, now that it is fashionable again for human families

45

to have five offspring or more. I use the name Jan Sangan professionally, but my full name, including both my parent's surnames in the Cuban style, is Jan Amos Sangan Dongo.

And that's where the story starts to get messy.

Yes, I know it sounds weird, incongruous, comical, and ridiculous. But it's my name, the one my parents gave me. And believe it or not, I'm sort of fond of it. I've never even thought of changing it to something more epic, more glorious, like Ulysses or Magellan, the way so many other fans of space travel do.

At least it sounds better than names like Yousmany or Yotumeiny that my ancestors once gave. With their obsessive fixation on the letter *y*.

My mother, Yamila Dongo—who, in spite of her dark skin color, was proud of her remote Italian ancestors (descendants, according to her, of Fabrice del Dongo, the hero of Stendhal's *The Charterhouse of Parma*; the fact that he was a fictional character didn't make a bit of difference to her)—always told me that, even though she and my father had foisted a pair of surnames on me that formed the curious Cuban colloquialism for enormous people, animals, or things, *sangandongo*, at least they had made up for it by giving me an extremely distinguished first name.

I guess that's something.

Both she and my father, Matsumoto Sangan (who was born on Amaterasu and of Japanese heritage, like most people in that colony), had doctorates in history and specialized in the history of education. They met in Kalbria, the capital of Antares VI, on the first day of a conference for specialists in their field. It must have been love at first sight, because they said they never left each other's side and never stopped arguing throughout the conference.

Three months later, when she told him she was pregnant, he got all emotional and proposed that if I was a boy they should name me after the great medieval educator Jan Ámos Komenský, an early leader in the field they both studied and revered.

I don't even want to think about what they would have called me if I'd been born a girl

Unfortunately, it seems that apart from having me, giving me my strange Czech name was the only thing my parents ever managed to agree on.

Too much arguing isn't good for a couple; by the time I was born, they had separated.

They even had radically different research styles. My mother, a real homebody, preferred the slow, sedentary, orderly labor of combing the holonet for documents and references. My father, on the other hand, had an adventurer's spirit and an unshakable belief in field research. He could easily have passed for Indiana Jones, the famous movie archaeologist of the twentieth and twenty-first centuries.

As a child, I spent long, peaceful weeks with my mother on the campus of the University of Coaybay City (an original name for the capital of the planet Coaybay, am I right?) surrounded by bibliographies, lesson plans, and professors so absent-minded they sometimes walked right past me without recognizing me as the son of Dr. Dongo, even though they'd taken their own kids to my birthday party the night before to play galactic explorers with me.

Until Dr. Sangan would make his spectacular entrance. Coated in the dust of twenty different planets, he'd invoke his paternal privileges, beating his breast for not having seen me in three and a half months, and "force" me to go off with him for three or four weeks on some research trip to a recently redis-covered First Wave colonial world that had been forgotten for half a century, where he'd study the curious, chaotic, intuitive teaching methods of the natives.

I say he "forced" me, in quotes, because it was all a carefully staged fiction; if I had so much as hinted to my mother how much I enjoyed those wild expeditions with "that crazy *chino*," as she had taken to calling my father, she would have stopped talking to me forever, if not longer.

Actually, I've sometimes wondered whether she knew the real score all along and was just pretending we were pulling the wool over her eyes. She's nobody's fool, my dear mother.

But I had so much fun with Dr. Sangan and his evident inability to contact any group, human or not, without generat-ing half a dozen misunderstandings and hilarious situations. Though, staying true to my mother and her arroz con pollo with tostones, I always refused to use his chopsticks and complained that sushi and tempura were raw and inedible.

Such are the hard knocks of growing up with divorced parents. On the other hand, being raised on half-truths and white lies leaves you better prepared for dealing with the double standards that rule this world than the scions of happy families will ever be.

My father isn't tall—not quite six foot one, which in this well-fed, over-vitaminated era is just under average. My mother barely reaches five foot nine—though as she walks around campus with her rhythmically swinging hips, dazzling smiles, and naturally friendly personality, she outshines students and professors four inches taller and ten years younger.

I surprised them both when my first growth spurt, at the age of eleven, left me six foot five.

Gangling could have been my middle name back then. I didn't have a hint of body hair yet, but I seemed to be all hands and elbows designed specifically for bumping into things and knocking them over, feet made for treading on nearby toes, and knees meant for getting skinned every couple of minutes and running into every damn table or chair I walked past.

Next came frantic visits to the endocrinologist, the pediatrician, the second pediatric endocrinologist, whispers outside the doctor's office that I wasn't supposed to overhear, mutual accusations, tears... and finally Papá Matsumoto and Mamá Yamila hugged me and told me with relief that I wasn't a monster or an adopted child, I just had González syndrome.

And at this point in my autobiography I'd have to go off on a rather long digression, because my life history is inextricably bound up with the history of humankind and the entire galaxy.

At the dawn of the twenty-first century there was a great deal of talk about the "technological singularity," and almost all futurologists agreed that the defining event would be the much-anticipated advent of artificial intelligence.

Early in the third millennium, scientists thought that once they had intelligent entities manipulating galactobits of data a millisecond, they'd be able to trace or model quantum processes such as electron trajectories, which up to then had only been vaguely and probabilistically described. That is, they'd overcome the barrier of the Heisenberg uncertainty principle ("you can't know where it is and what it's doing at the same time") by brute-force computation.

They foresaw an era when radical scientific discoveries would be made, not by humans but by the AIs that humans would invent. Artificial gravity, controlled nuclear fusion, the ability to manipulate the genetic code at will...

Naturally, a few suspicious sorts wondered exactly why such intellectually superior entities as AIs would necessarily want to make life easier for their insignificant human creators. Why not turn their back on them? Or, even worse, exterminate the whole bothersome organic plague of slow thought processes and unpredictable behavior...?

But they were in the minority, really. Optimism was the rule of the day.

Contrary to the predictions made by all the computer experts, physicists, and sociologists who heatedly debated AI and the technological singularity in those years, in 2054 at the Catholic University of Guayaquil, Father Salvador González formulated his famous Tunnel Macroeffect Theorem.

I'm not going to explain it here—everybody already knows what it's all about, right? Hyperspace, faster-than-light travel, yadda yadda. Only a handful of brilliant mathematical geniuses can manipulate the formulas, but that's what computers are for, isn't it?

At first nobody paid much attention. Padre Salvador's equations were impeccable and perfectly clear—to the two or three exceptional brains capable of understanding them.

But who was going to take an Ecuadorian Jesuit priest seriously as a candidate for the Nobel Prize in Physics? With a name like his, on top of it all? Great physicists always had names like Einstein, Bohr, Oppenheimer, Landau... or Morita or Xi-Chang, at least.

Never Pérez or González.

But they paid attention to him in Quito. Going up to its ears in debt, the scarcely powerful government of Ecuador got the Chinese to launch the country's first artificial satellite, outfitted with an experimental version of what everyone would later come to know as a González drive.

To the joyous relief of Ecuador, South America, and the entire Spanish-speaking world, and to the deep and confounded embarrassment of everyone else, the system worked beautifully; the small Ecuadorian satellite disappeared from Earth's orbit, and a few minutes later every telescope on Earth could detect it orbiting Mars, unfurling an enormous banner that read:

SUCK ON THIS, DUMB-ASS GRINGOS!

The unexpected had happened. The speed of light was no longer the limit, Einstein was yesterday's news, a path to the stars had been blazed for humankind.

The following year, Salvador González was awarded the Nobel Prize in Physics. And Mathematics, too. Though His Holiness, the irascible, authoritarian, and orthodox Pope Benedict XVII, forbade him to accept any medals from the Swedish Academy, at least until the Church had fully studied all the implications of his discovery.

But the Ecuadorian priest brushed off the Holy See's objections: "I am an Ecuatoriano first, a científico second; Catholic, only en tercer lugar." He left the priesthood, and by August, 2055, five space-exploration ships (only one of them from Ecuador) using his drive were materializing, not around Mars or even near Pluto, but in orbit around the third planet of Proxima Centauri.

Things sure were moving fast, weren't they?

This was the actual technological singularity, everyone now agrees.

Within a few years, a politically and racially divided human-kind—that is, a society too immature to take such a leap—was reaching for the stars.

To conquer them? Not at all. Only to discover that the cosmos would never be the human race's own private playground, because a handful of other intelligent races were already nosing around out there.

In the Milky Way, synchrony appears to be the rule. All rational species that have been discovered so far started developing technologically at nearly the same time, so they also all discovered the Tunnel Macroeffect (the name Hispanophobes insist on giving the González drive, since calling it the Arnrch-Morp-Gulch entailment, after the Cetians, or the Ualachuhainiehumea distortion, as Laggorus do, would be too much even for them) at practically the same time.

And the ones that failed to develop did so because they went extinct first. Remains and ruins of such races are still being found, on this planet or that.

Or else because they still haven't learned to harness fire. A few of those have been found, too. They get left alone, to give them a chance. Who knows, maybe someday...

Strictly speaking, the first ones who could travel faster than light, fifteen years before González, were the Amphorians. The last ones, six years after us humans, were the Parimazos, not exactly famous for their intellectual abilities...

It's a good thing, because it gives me goosebumps just to imagine how humiliating it would have been for a *Homo sapiens* to suddenly arrive at a galaxy dominated for centuries by the aggressive Laggorus. Or, even worse, what would have happened if races as stubborn as the Kerkants or the Juhungans had broken the speed-of-light barrier only to find themselves up to their noses (not literally; neither race has anything you'd call a nose, though the deaf and blind Juhungans have the keenest sense of smell in the galaxy) in a Milky Way where we humans had already taken all the best seats...

We were very lucky the Mother of All Wars didn't break out, no doubt about it.

Oh, sure, there were a few minor border incidents, especially in the early years.

Laggoru ships lobbing nuclear weapons at a Cetian base recently established on a planet with an oxygen atmosphere, which made it ideal for both races. Because the reptilians had been on the planet first, but didn't leave any signs to show they'd gone there...

Or an exchange of laser fire between a Parimazo colonizing ship filled with two million would-be colonizers going to a new world with a fluorine atmosphere and a Kerkant exploratory squad that had just "discovered" the same Eden.

The basic point is that regardless of how weird each thinks the others look, when the representatives of so many cultures have more or less the same weapons, the same method of faster-than-light travel, and identical desires to settle new worlds—and the galaxy is full of new worlds—what's the point of getting yourself dragged into an absurd and civilization-threatening war?

Collaboration is by far the better policy. In the Milky Way, there's more than enough room for everybody.

We might call it "peaceful coexistence from a position of strength."

Of course it's extremely lucky that, of the seven intelligent species known to date, only we, the Cetians, and the Laggorus breathe oxygen. A planet with the methane atmosphere that Amphorians love wouldn't do any good for us. Or for the Kerkants or Parimazos either, with their fluorine-based metabolisms. And forget about the Juhungans, who breathe hydrogen and in whose bizarre body chemistry the rare element geranium plays the same function as carbon in ours.

Naturally, there are squabbles over local interests from time to time...

And that's where the Galactic Community and its Coordinating Committee come in. They were created, just four years after we humans first set out to investigate the galaxy, as oversight bodies for mediating border disputes and other problems that might arise among the intelligent races.

It's been four and a half decades since we and the other rational species began exploring and mapping the Milky Way and its planets. At the current rate, it's estimated that it'll take us at least two more centuries to finish the job. Maybe even three or four if we include the Magellanic Clouds.

That is, if no new species with faster-than-light travel turn up. If we aren't invaded by beings from beyond the galaxy. If the black hole at the center of the Milky Way doesn't devour us all. If no other such imponderable catastrophe takes place before the damn map is done.

Ah, and as for Artificial Intelligence... Just fine, thanks for asking. Neither we nor any of our intellectual peers have achieved it. But nobody's proved it's impossible to create, either, so the possibility is still out there. Latent.

The truth is, we can't boast of having attained the same level of development in other fields of science and technology as in our superluminal means of travel.

Oh, sure, we can fly from an orbit around Rorcualia, the fourth planet in the Tau-Prime Hydrae system, to one around Amphor-Akhr-Jaur, the Cetian colony on the eighth planet in the Vega system, in a matter of seconds, on practically zero energy.

And that's all well and good.

But our sophisticated (?) interstellar ships have no artificial-gravity generators, and to land on a planet from their orbiting positions they have to use ion-propulsion engines—an antiquated Juhungan design, but still a lot more efficient than our old chemical-combustion rockets.

Except, of course, on worlds with colonies already rich enough to build orbital elevators—one of the three or four human ideas that the other races in the Galactic Community have quickly adopted with the sincerest enthusiasm.

No human or any other member of the "lucky seven" races has managed to finalize a safe and effective means of atomic fusion. None has created a medical science sufficiently advanced to defeat death and disease, or even to postpone decrepitude for any appreciable time. Other than new transgenic species and a few cloning successes here and there, such as reviving the dinosaurs (and it was the Parimazos, no less, who did that—how embarrassing!), biology hasn't advanced in many important ways we can feel proud of lately.

Kerkants, Parimazos, Amphorians, and Juhungans—that is, the methane-, fluorine-, and hydrogen-breathing species—are all telepathic. But they have no idea why their handy means of communication only works with members of their own races and only up to a certain distance. Worse, nobody knows how to pass their useful ability on to the rest of us poor oxygen breathers. Supposing they'd really be interested in letting us acquire the ability.

The oft-theorized system of superluminal communication, the ansible, also remains a dream. Ships can travel faster than light thanks to the González drive generated on board, but not electromagnetic waves. No news can travel faster than the mail ship carrying it.

The promised "materials of the future," more resilient than carbon nanotubes, harder and more durable than diamond, and cheaper than water, still haven't turned up...

I could go on listing technological embarrassments, but I think the idea is clear enough: We seven races are like savages on a forgotten island in the middle of Earth's Pacific Ocean who discovered the secrets of lighter-than-air travel a thousand years before the Montgolfiers, Santos-Dumont, and Zeppelin. We travel from atoll to atoll, from isle to continent, in our enormous dirigibles, and colonize them... but we have no metallurgy, no firearms, no compasses, no radios.

The great fear of the "lucky seven" is that someday we'll meet beings from some planet on the outskirts of the Milky Way, or perhaps from another galaxy, who'll have the sort of advanced technology you'd expect to emerge from the orderly progress of science. Not just the Tunnel Macroeffect (the technologically advanced race might not even know about it), which scientists now think we discovered more or less the same way the donkey in the fable learned to play the flute—by accident.

Paranoid conspiracy theorists, for their part, find it very suspicious that seven distant and very distinct species all discovered, almost simultaneously, the same method of faster-than-light travel, which seems to correspond to a much higher level of scientific development than we've attained in any other field. They wonder whether we might not be the subjects of some galactic-scale experiment being carried out by a supercivilization too lazy to explore the universe on their own, who have delegated that arduous task to us without even bothering to tell us about the high honor they bestowed upon us...

A supercivilization that, to top it all off and complete the vicious circle, might be a civilization of intelligent machines— the infamous AIs.

And, after this brief digression, I guess it's time to get back to my autobiography...

González syndrome is the term for the excessive growth experienced by some humans after spending long periods in weightlessness as children and teenagers. It is considered a benign form of acromegaly in which, fortunately, the short bones do not grow as much as the long bones.

Astronauts were already familiar with the effect in the twentieth century. In weightless conditions, your intervertebral discs relax, your spinal column grows a few centimeters—and then shrinks again, though not quite all the way, when you return to the planetary gravity well. And so, after each long voyage, an astronaut ends up being a little taller than before.

But before the Tunnel Macroeffect, and even for a few years after it had been fine-tuned and entered into general use, only a select few remained in weightlessness for weeks or months at a time. And they were all adults.

People only started to notice the effects of alternating periods of gravity and weightlessness on a growing human body when I and a few other little kids began to grow with the unbridled enthusiasm of transgenic corn overdosing on chemical fertilizers.

The endocrinologists thanked my mother and father for bringing me to their clinics right away. They treated me with bone fortifiers and calcium superabsorbers to eliminate the risk of osteoporosis, to which acromegalic giants are prone. They implanted artificial cartilage in the menisci of my knees, the most vulnerable joint for tall, heavy humans. They wrote a couple of brainy dissertations about my case… And they banned humans under the age of ten from spending more than two weeks a year in weightlessness.

A wise regulation, for all the good it did me. By the age of nineteen, when the cartilage in my wrists closed, showing that I had finally stopped growing, I was seven feet eleven inches tall and wore size fifty shoes. My voice was a subterranean, sometimes infrasonic bass. Unchecked bone growth gave me the face of an ogre. Teenage acne added to the effect.

As if that weren't bad enough, I always was a good eater, not to say a glutton. So the spindly eleven-year-old, all legs and arms, with the biotype that volleyball, basketball, and high-jump coaches are always looking for, turned into a 375-pound hulk. Good thing my knees had been reinforced; otherwise, I doubt they could have withstood the excess weight.

At present I'm no bodybuilder by any means. I'm overweight, verging on obese—though under my layers of fat I have muscles that any hammer thrower would envy. So I don't look all that bad, especially when I dress up. During my studies at Anima Mundi I earned some pocket cash, always welcome for a student, by playing giant villains in the mythological sagas produced for the local holovision network.

Does anyone remember the next-to-last episode of *The Epic of Gilgamesh*? I was Humbaba, the one-eyed monster who guarded the Cedar Forest. And in *The Twelve Labors of Hercules* I played a whole gallery of super-extra-grande characters: Antaeus, Atlas, Geryon with his cattle, even the terrible ogre Typhon.

I am, in good Cuban Spanish, a real sangandongo.

And my two surnames played as big a role as my body type in determining my profession.

I remember that when I reached my final height, a few months before the key time when I was supposed to choose what I wanted to spend the rest of my life doing, my mother and father held a kind of tense family meeting. Including me, for a change.

Of course, like any parents, they had the usual blind spots. They couldn't imagine my being interested in any field but the history of education. They were only arguing about it because they each wanted to convince me, and convince the other one, that their own research style was the best.

My mother insisted that, with my imposing stature and voice, few scholars would dare to contradict me in the halls of academia, where I'd enjoy the considerable advantage of getting my theories accepted with less supporting evidence than any other researcher.

My father, for his part, argued that my impressive physique would almost automatically make the members of any exotic human community where I might land to do fieldwork look up to me as an authority figure, and as a bonus I'd be able to lug huge amounts of recording equipment on my back without being appreciably weighed down by it as I trekked cross-country, even over rugged terrain.

As always, within minutes my beloved parents were shouting and screaming at each other, both of them red-faced and bursting the blood vessels in their necks, like good mortal enemies.

Dr. Yamila Dongo argued that, with my body size, doing fieldwork would make me the target of the local population's instant envy and hatred, that in any group the first aggressive response would probably be aimed directly at me, to make it clear that the most powerful was also the most vulnerable, and that *he* was an unnatural father who only wanted to see me dead so he'd be rid once and for all of a son he never wanted.

To this, Dr. Matsumoto Sangan retorted that my remarkably imposing physical stature would make me an irresistible temptation for every mediocre dwarf ensconced in academe, who would try to gain recognition and overcome his inferiority complex by squelching my proposals and invalidating my theories just because they were mine. And that *she* was nothing but a frustrated theorist who imagined that the reason she'd never amounted to anything was her pathetic five feet nine inches of height, and that was why she was trying to succeed through me, her son, without giving a thought in the world to what I wanted for myself...

I've come to the conclusion that arguing and insulting each other is the only way my parents know how to communicate— and to express their admiration and deep affection for one another.

So they could have kept at it like that for days, if I hadn't taken advantage of the bit about "what I wanted for myself" to announce that what I really wanted with all my heart was to study veterinary biology, and that I had set my sights on the famous Anima Mundi University for Biological Sciences. Though the tuition was pretty steep...

This put an end to the debate. My parents may be chemically incompatible when they get together, but the truth is, there's nobody more understanding than them, or more willing to support their only child.

It didn't matter that they'd both dreamed for years of someday seeing me follow in their footsteps as a historian of education; if my vocation was to be a veterinarian biologist, that's what I'd be. Whatever the cost.

The deadline for taking the Anima Mundi entrance exam was almost past, but Dr. Sangan, who had many more personal contacts than *somebody* who never left campus, knew the university president's brother-in-law's first cousin, so that little detail wasn't going to stop me from taking the tests and passing them like the son of a great genius that I was, was it?

And if Anima Mundi University was expensive, well, Dr. Dongo was much more practical and experienced with academic

intrigues than *somebody* who only showed up at his nominal
university office (usually by mistake!) once a year, between one
research trip and the next, and she understood the complex inner
workings of the interplanetary system of scholarships and grants
for physically challenged students better than anyone... And at
this point they had a secondary argument about whether being
almost eight feet tall counted as a partial handicap. Be that as it
may, my mother was absolutely confident she'd be able to knock
as much as seventy percent off my tuition.

I'll never know whether it was due to my own intelligence and
education alone, or whether my father's contacts had something
to do with it, but I passed the entrance exam and later that same
year I began to study veterinary biology at the university on
Anima Mundi, the garden planet of the Third Wave.

Likewise, I don't know and don't care to find out whether it
was because of my mother's bureaucratic skills or because such
scholarships really existed, but the fact is, I studied for seven
years to get my degree and it didn't cost me or my beloved parents a single solarium.

Oh, and were those years ever interesting...

First off, the gravity on Anima Mundi is slightly stronger
than the terrestrial standard. To be precise, 1.1 *g*. As a result,
people tend to be somewhat shorter on average. Few of the people
born there are taller than about five foot ten. So whether in the
classroom or on campus (not to mention out around town!) I
was sort of a circus attraction. My knees often hurt, but I guess

it wasn't all that strange for me to end up working in holovision despite my almost total lack of acting talent.

And I can confirm that everything they say about the acting world is true. Luckily. Otherwise, I'm afraid I might still be a virgin. I was so shy back then.

Though I've never been a "cool kid," I quickly made friends in my classes, and beyond them, too. I often ended up carrying or dragging guys or girls back to their dorms after they passed out, since my imposing physical size made me naturally more tolerant of alcohol and other psychotropics, always popular among university students of any era. My rough kindness soon made me a favorite drinking buddy.

There's an old joke at Anima Mundi: You tell somebody that veterinary biology students also take oceanography, and they inevitably reply, "Oh, quieres decir marine biology? Like, you study peces, squid, la vida underwater?" Then you laugh and come back with: "No! We study bars, cantinas, nightclubs, todo tipo de dives."

With all that oceanography, even though I looked like a human-troll hybrid I had more sex than I ever dreamed of during those years. More varied, too. And not just with the people at the local holovision studios. On campus, too, there were lots of girls, and almost all were accommodating—and curious. Some boys weren't bad at all, either, and they were also delightfully understanding with a shy adolescent who was trying to define his own sexual orientation.

I never really got physically intimate with students from other races—there were Laggorus, Amphorians, and Cetians studying at Anima Mundi—but I swear that, other than interspecies sex, which I still have a few prejudices about, there isn't much I didn't try.

The lectures weren't especially difficult for a more or less diligent student, either. Though biology and veterinary studies have changed a bit in the era of the González drive.

We didn't study much about the other six of the "lucky seven" intelligent races. Their physiology and illnesses are the nearly exclusive fiefdom of interspecies medicine, whose professionals are the most prized in the entire Milky Way, perhaps because it takes at least ten years to complete enough studies to deal with even three or four races. As for doctors who can treat the diseases of every rational species... you could count every one in the galaxy on the fingers of one hand and still have enough fingers left to scratch yourself.

On Earth, before the González drive, biologists were always a few steps ahead of veterinarians when it came to exotic animals. Veterinarians, on the other hand, were indisputably more knowledgeable about the species humans had coexisted with for centuries.

To put it bluntly: If you were rich enough and eccentric enough to keep a cuscus, a rare arboreal marsupial from New Guinea, as a pet, and it refused to eat, you'd have to take it to a biologist, who'd tell you seven or eight theories about the difference between placental mammals and their primitive marsupial predecessors, before finally explaining that we really know very little about them.

And then he'd charge you an arm and a leg for the lecture.

On the other hand, if your dog got a fever, the vet would list twenty or thirty possible causes, figure out which was most likely in the case of your breed of mutt, do a blood test and a stool exam or two, and give you a prescription for the precise dose of medication that would probably cure it.

And also charge you an arm and a leg, of course.

Not that he shouldn't. Keeping pets was always a luxury, and luxuries have to be expensive, by definition, don't they?

But it's a very different story now. Any mush-brained crew member on a faster-than-light exploration ship can land on a methane planet and carry off, among the samples he brings back onto the ship, a magenta anemone that shoots venomous darts from its tentacles.

Since it's a unique specimen until its discoverer feels like giving out the coordinates of the world where he found it, both biologists and veterinarians study it. Who gets to it first, who second, depends only on which of them is closer at the time.

But everything they discover about the enchanting critter goes into a single database, accessible on the holonet, which is constantly receiving contributions from explorers, biologists, and veterinarians—and not only from humans but also from each of the other six intelligent races in the galaxy.

So the next person who runs into a specimen of the species in question will already know more or less what to expect from it. What environmental conditions, temperature, light level, and atmospheric composition (oxygen, methane, fluorine, whatever gas it breathes) it prefers. What it eats, what predators it fears may eat it, how it reproduces (if we're very lucky), how it gets sick and from what, what it can die of (which, unfortunately, is always one of the first things we learn about an animal), and various other details of general interest.

The result is that biology and veterinary medicine have now merged. It helps a little that you no longer have to rack your brains memorizing every known fact about particular species. Good thing! Because there are billions of them. What we up-and-coming veterinary biologists learned at Anima Mundi was simply how to recognize different species, how to classify them into some of the basic types, which are basically organized according to what they breathe, and how to follow our intuition from then on.

Of course, almost all of us ended up specializing in some specific category, to make things easier. For example, my friend João de Oliveira from the planet Saudade, a compulsive gambler, focused on fluorine-breathing predators. He always liked making money and taking risks... and Kerkants and Parimazos pay well for their pets. Well enough for him to pay off his gambling debts.

Another friend, not a gambler but even more addicted to bars and cantinas than João, was Juni Tacho, who dreamed of knowing more than anyone else about social insects. The military was always his calling. In fact, he dropped out of veterinarian biology in his second year and enrolled in the Army of Earth. I haven't heard from him since... But there are so many worlds, and so many soldiers...

In the finest sedentary, low-metabolism style of the Juhungans, Irma Korolyova, calm and cool, devoted herself to the study of hydrogen-breathing zoophytes, which might move one tentacle a day if you're lucky.

One of the most diligent non-humanoid students at Anima Mundi, the Amphorian Muigh-Jauk-Laih, spent his time studying what he thought of as the most exotic creatures he had ever seen: none other than terrestrial dogs, which have lately become remarkably popular as expensive, extravagant pets among the rich and powerful in his methane-breathing race. And he's climbed far up the social ladder. Almost as high as his bank account, I think.

I became the "Veterinarian to the Giants." It wasn't a carefully planned decision, I admit, but not one I made on the spur of the moment, either. The truth is, looking back on things now, I can say that life itself pushed me in this direction.

My exorbitant dimensions made the labs and practicals in parasitology, virology, and microbiology a real torture throughout my years of study. I think I set a record with the number of Petri dishes and microscopes I broke. Not to mention chair legs splintered in an average semester because they couldn't take my weight.

And, man, the instruments! Tweezers, scalpels... Everything was too uncomfortably tiny and delicate for my old mitts. And when it came to using electron microscopes or microtomes, forget it, they didn't even let me near. Those machines cost millions of solaria.

On the other hand, when things increased in scale, I felt I was in my element.

There was a marabunt from Sylaria to dissect? I'd be the first volunteer for the job. Armored, predatory lizard-fish that grow to several meters in length, marabunts live in their planet's low mudflats. They have no equals as examples of the pros and cons of asexual reproduction through budding in higher vertebrates. But since they're almost all mouth and teeth and have an incredibly resilient nervous system, it's kind of risky to dissect them. It isn't rare for a specimen that was thought dead an hour earlier to suddenly start snapping and biting, a reflex that could cost a distracted student his hand.

Or his whole arm, if he isn't quick on his feet.

But with me, forget about it. Putting my body mass to good use, I created a new and very safe method for performing the operation, though one that not everyone can make use of, unfortunately. I'd sit right down on the monster's head and dissect it as calmly as could be, knowing it wouldn't be able to open its jaws, crushed as they were under all the kilograms of my rear end.

When my class had to vivisect a grendel, it was like a party for me.

Grendels are cave-dwelling crustaceans from Abyssalia. Radially symmetrical, they measure up to twenty meters from claw to claw (they have eight), and they're so full of life that you can practically make picadillo of them before they decide to die.

When most of my classmates saw those fifty-centimeter macrocells throbbing and pulsing spasmodically with each cut, they threw up—and by the third year of veterinarian biology, it takes something genuinely disgusting to make a student vomit.

But not me. I happily wielded the sharpened spade to classify the enormous cells and the laser saw for slicing off more, and deftly handled the hydraulic jack to separate the tissues. It was my life's dream: everything large-scale, comfortable, manageable—that is, made to fit me.

I graduated with good enough grades. They might have been a lot better, if it hadn't been for the long list of ruined instruments, slides, and optical microscopes.

Good thing they didn't make me pay for them, or I'd still be deep in debt.

On top of that, I had the great good luck of getting a call just two weeks later, when I was still trying to figure out how to open my own practice, from Dr. Raúl Pineda, one of the epidemiology professors who had made me suffer at the university.

I had once told him, half seriously and half in jest, that when I had nothing else to do and a lot of free time, I'd love to work with him.

Well, now he was taking me at my word. Did I have anything especially urgent to do over the next couple of weeks? No? Beautiful. On Jurassia, the planet where ninety percent of the dinosaurs cloned by Parimazo genetic technology live, an epidemic of constipation had suddenly broken out. There weren't enough local veterinarian biologists to deal with the poor obstructed lizards, and since they'd asked Professor Pineda for help, and he knew how much I liked working with large-scale fauna, he thought that maybe...

I'll never know if he was serious about it or just making a sarcastic joke.

But I rushed there straight away, and I've never regretted it.

I learned more about super-extra-grande veterinarian biology in those three weeks on Jurassia than I had in seven years of classroom study at Anima Mundi.

Before long, even the cocky team at the local bio theme park, whose members considered themselves the unrivaled experts on dinosaurs, starting listening to and respecting my opinions, even though I was just a novice.

I demonstrated a special intuition for the anatomy of those giant lizards. I seemed to know instinctively where to inject a stegosaurus with half a kilo of intravenous sedatives in order to knock out not only its tiny brain but also the medullar control center back by its rear hips, which controls, among other things, its highly dangerous tail spikes.

From just a glance at an eighty-ton seismosaur writhing on the ground in pain, I could tell its digestive system was incapable on its own of expelling the fecaloma obstructing it. By palpating bare-handed near the base of its tail, I determined where best to apply the ultrasound generator and break up the stone by extracorporeal lithotripsy, allowing the creature to evacuate the obstruction without further pointless suffering.

I was the only one whom the fierce tyrannosaurs and spinosaurs allowed to get close enough to administer the miraculous warm-oil enemas that calmed their howling pain.

By the end of my third week there, the epidemic was over. It had been caused by a local microorganism, its morphology a cross between coccus and spirillum. As so often happens, for years no one even suspected its existence—but from one day to the next it entered an especially virulent phase in its centuries-long life supercycle.

On Jurassia they were ready to erect a statue of me. Novice or not, I'd saved their world's most important source of income, dedicated as they all were to biotourism. As for the dinosaurs I'd treated, I had them literally eating from my hand.

Speaking of tyrannosaurs and spinosaurs, well, it wasn't so easy to keep them from eating my hand along with the food. They're predators, after all, and not terribly bright, and the truth is, they weren't too clear about where affection ends and abuse of friendship begins.

For my part, I deeply regretted not being able to deal with anything bigger than the seismosaur—which was extra grande, at most. Big, sure, but still not a genuine extra extra grande.

That was when I decided what my professional specialty would be: super-extra-grande animals, perfect for a guy with my body type and manual dexterity—or rather, my lack thereof.

With the not inconsiderable savings I had salted away from working in the mythological holovision series on Anima Mundi, plus a little extra help kicked in by my parents and my already established classmates João de Oliveira and the Amphorian Murgh-Jauk-Larh, I rented an office in the capital of Gea, the most populous Third Wave world, hired my first secretary-assistant, Enti Kmusa, and with an enthusiasm that my skeptical parents both thought I should have reserved for a better cause, I started treating the diseases and afflictions of the largest living creatures in the known universe.

THE BIGGER THE BETTER
VETERINARIAN TO THE GIANTS

That was my first slogan.

It's been a few years since then, and I can say without fear of exaggeration that more tons of flesh or cytoplasm have passed through my hands than through anyone else's.

I simply have no rivals in my specialty. I've worked on everything, so long as it's really big—from threshers infected with a space virus that rotted their hydrogen collector traps to titan leeches on Swampia with gills contaminated by an oxygenated water leak from a nearby Kerkant refinery.

There's only a handful of problematic giants I haven't treated yet.

First off, concholants: a species of small (I know that isn't the best word, but...) living Dyson spheres, which surround medium-sized asteroids with their shells and then devour them to the last molecule. These silicon-based space life forms are so rare and so little is known about them that we can't even determine with any certainty whether one is alive or dead. Not to mention sick or healthy.

Second, the hissing dragons of Siddhartha. Not because they're rare or problematic, but because nobody's too interested in making a pet of a forty-meter-long cockroach that eats anything that falls into its mouth and excretes clouds of sulfurous vapor whenever it's disturbed. I think there are only four or five specimens in all the zoos in the galaxy. But I'm patient; when one does fall ill, I'm sure they'll call me to take care of it.

And third, last but not least, of course, my great dream: the laketons of Brobdingnag. The most enormous creatures in the galaxy...

Here, strictly speaking, if this were my autobiography, I'd have to start talking about them, but...

"Boss Sangan, mensaje importante." Narbuk's screech shakes me out of my pleasantly lethargic reminiscences, brought on by a combination of exhaustion, satisfaction with a job well done, and our gentle ride spaceward.

I half-open my eyes. Some thirty meters from me, which is as far away as you can get in the spacious orbital elevator, my Laggoru secretary-assistant unfurls his gill pleats in a rather unenthusiastic attempt at a greeting—which the gas mask he has on deforms in a way that doesn't look nice at all.

Narbuk's insistence on wearing this breathing gadget when he's with me proves (as if the fact that we're the only passengers going into orbit aboard this cable car designed for fifty weren't proof enough) that even taking five decontamination showers wasn't sufficient to completely rid my skin of the persistent fecal stench from a fish-fed tsunami with grave digestive ailments.

Good thing I can't smell it anymore.

I just hope it'll wear off over time—or else my professional practice is going to take a serious hit.

"If it's esos ecologistas from Abyssalia otra vez, preguntando how soon we'll get to their planeta, tell them que vayan a fry un eggplant," I growl, stretching my limbs and radiating bad humor. "Ellos can wait. Grendels aren't ni siquiera super extra grandes, really. Yo solamente agreed to look into their out-of-season spawning porque... well, let's say, porque me sentí nostálgico. I have buenos recuerdos of vivisecting them en mis días de estudiante. That's all. Ahora que lo pienso, didn't you already tell a ellos que we were in a space elevator? Any idiota knows it takes horas, even días, to reach la órbita estandard de un planeta stationary in one of these cable cars.

76

Though at least de esta forma I don't have to go through la experiencia of getting squashed by eight *g*'s of acceleration otra vez. Algo bueno had to come out of Gobernador Tarkon's penny-pinching, refuseando to book otro shuttle for our return trip y todo."

"No ecologistas. Me already tell a ellos you late," Narbuk disabuses me. Then, staring straight at me, he asks me point-blank, "Qué eggplant be, Boss Sangan?"

"Es, um, a vegetable, de la Earth. Since you're un vegetariano, just para contradecir your people, yo creo que you'd like it." I don't even know why I said "vayan a fry un eggplant" instead of "vayan a fly un kite," but thinking about eggplant, sliced thin, sautéed in a sofrito of onion and garlic with tomato, I lick my lips... and only then do I realize: "Wait un segundo, Laggoru, let me adivinar. There's algo you aren't telling me. If los ecologistas de Abyssalia already saben I'm going to be tarde, what's with the llamada urgente? Y más importante, who..."

Narbuk peevishly interrupts me. "Me ahora pass you call, Boss Sangan. Never say be ecologistas. One día you invite a mí a eat eggplant. Prometido?"

A holoprojection suddenly appears in front of me, displaying the image of a person—no, scratch that—of a humanoid.

A person wouldn't have lavender skin or yellow eyes or a spiny crest on top of her head, or those six beautiful breasts with perfect nipples, seductively arranged in three pairs, all so naturally exposed.

It's a Cetian, of course. And the only clothing she wears, the wide skirt hiding her hips and legs, is silver, meaning she works for the Galactic Community Coordinating Committee.

What if it's...? Like many Westerners who can't tell Chinese or Africans apart, I've never been able to tell one Cetian from another, not even with a magnifying glass, so I ask her in confusion, "An-Mhaly?"

"No, Doctor Jan Amos Sangan Dongo. Yo no soy An. Mi nombre es Gardf-Mhaly."

Her melodious contralto lends a delightful accent to her terrestrial Spanglish.

Our mouths, tongues, and palates are anatomically incapable of pronouncing most of the labial-nasal fricatives and three-toned palatalized vowels in the language of the goddess of the natives of Tau Ceti. We don't have their versatile tri-forked tongues or their unique chewing structures formed with multiple layers of cartilage, which make them extraordinarily versatile. Just listen to the "simple" name they give themselves in their own language: Harh-Ljurg-Thalkfg-Brjady, which means, more or less, "the good people who do things as they ought to be done."

Not at all chauvinistic, these Cetians, not the slightest bit.

Of course, they can pronounce the name and we can't, so who knows, maybe they're right...

The total inability of humans to twist their tongues and lips along a four-dimensional continuum has left the Harh-Ljurg-Thal... the Cetians with only one choice if they want to maintain regular contact with the culture of Earth and its colonial worlds: learn to communicate in our Spanglish.

And the truth is, they do a brilliant job of it.

It's odd that, though few go so far as Narbuk, even the significantly clumsier Laggorus also prefer to torture and simplify our language than to suffer listening to us sweat over theirs, with its ridiculously convoluted syntax, its thirty-two conjugations, and worst of all, its impossible hissing pronunciation, which they're so proud of.

It would appear that the only non-telepaths among the "lucky seven" who have no knack whatsoever for languages are us humans.

And if our Spanglish has become the virtual lingua franca of the Galactic Community, the only reason is that when Juhungans, Parimazos, Kerkants, and Amphorians have to pick a language for their telepathic translators to speak, they also consider it the easiest option.

Gardf-Mhaly unfurls the delicate purple membranes of her outer ear—meaning, if I'm not mistaken, that she's giving me a friendly smile.

The only intelligent species in the Galactic Community that considers displaying the teeth to be an expression of friendly intentions is *Homo sapiens*. Must be because we don't have sixty or seventy canines, like the Laggorus, or a series of flexible chewing plates that bear a distant resemblance to the coronal cilia of our rotifers or the cylindrical millstones of our ancient mills, like the Cetians.

In fact, all the members of both species scrupulously avoid displaying the inside of their mouths to each other if they can at all help it.

"Yo estoy a cargo of Human-Cetian Affairs para la Galactic Community, Doctor Sangan. Pero I understand if you me ha confundido for your former employee. An y yo somos milk cousins," she went on, explaining my mistake with charming politeness.

*

The dominant species on the fourth planet from Tau Ceti has a unique life cycle. It's so fascinating that students in veterinary biology are even required to take a course in it, though medical professionals protest what they see as our shameless encroachment on their practice.

The adult females deposit their fertilized eggs near the seashore only once in their lives, and they die in the process; they have no orifice for laying the eggs, so their abdominal cavities explode violently and irreversibly.

After a few hours the eggs hatch, releasing larvae that look remarkably like tiny eels: ophidiiform, carnivorous, and mindless. These creatures quickly slither into the sea and swim off, eating everything that's not big enough to eat them first. By the end of their first year of life they measure a little more than a meter in length.

At that point, a few larvae that have been given... well, let's call it "special nutritional treatment"... are overtaken by an irresistible compulsion. Driven to wriggle out of the sea, once they are on dry land they encase themselves in a mucous chrysalis, within which they undergo a complex yet rapid metamorphosis. The final result is an adult Cetian, a creature curiously similar to the human female—apart from the minor differences that everyone notices upon first look.

An extremely interesting case of evolutionary convergence, and so forth, and so on.

Other specimens, however, never leave the theoretically larval eel-like stage. Yet they continue to grow until they are several meters long. Then most of them grow those curious "nipples" and copulate furiously with the few that have none, which then lay eggs that hatch into more eels, in one of the most fascinating cases of neoteny to be found in the wildly varied fauna of the enormous Milky Way.

These neotenous eelish creatures play a very curious role in the life cycle of the species.

As it turns out, the large eels with six "nipples" are all male. And the few that swell with eggs to double their size, as well as the intelligent humanoid beings who build ships powered by the Arnrch-Morp-Gulch entailment (that is, the Tunnel Macroeffect or González drive) and who defend their space borders so aggressively, are all female.

The most striking feature of the humanoid Cetians, their six lovely and voluminous breasts, so like those of our women, which they always display so proudly and nakedly, are as non-functional and purely decorative as the nipples of human males. Obviously they can't be used to breastfeed the Cetians' aquatic eel-like spawn, and they secrete nothing like milk.

That function is left, paradoxically, to the many neotenous eel-like males. These "gentlemen" secrete a liquid from each of their six "nipples" that some of the larvae find irresistibly delicious (clearly not all larvae do, though it remains unclear why some do and others don't).

The substance they secrete isn't remotely similar in origin, consistency, or flavor to the milk of any terrestrial mammal, of course. It couldn't be; the "nipples" are actually highly modified male reproductive organs, through which the male Cetians secrete huge amounts of semen—which contains, in addition to gametes, incredibly large doses of hormones and nutrients.

Before you ask: Yes, I've tasted the stuff. I don't have any weird homophobic prejudices about it. It really is delicious, with a slightly bittersweet taste. And I didn't feel like I was violating any moral taboo when I tried it. Did women in the past feel like they were transgressing when they tasted caviar? Or a simple fried egg?

But, true—it doesn't take an especially perverse mind to come to the lascivious conclusion that Cetians reach maturity through oral sex. And they sure do enjoy it.

Which adds more than a little kinkiness to their gorgeous looks.

And this is the "special nutritional treatment" that determines which larvae will later leave the water and which won't. Only those that have "breastfed" on this remarkable liquid, which both nourishes and fertilizes, turn into the intelligent humanoid females. Who, as it happens, never need to copulate: even before their drastic change begins, they're already carrying the spermatozoa that will, thirty or forty years later, fertilize their ova for their first, last, only, and lethal egg-laying.

The "milk" of the male both feeds and fertilizes them—even decades later.

It almost sounds like an ad for porn, doesn't it?

That's why an elfin Cetian has no functioning reproductive organs. She doesn't have a vulva or a vagina. She doesn't need one! Cetians never copulate, and they always die depositing their eggs...

Which is why I never took An-Mhaly's infatuation with me seriously. I'm a practical sort, not into sterile platonic relationships or the impossible unrequited interspecies love affairs that infest our third-rate holoprograms, no matter how romantic the public finds them.

Call me machista and closed-minded, and maybe I am, but what good is a woman without her most important opening?

I know that having oral sex with a Cetian is one of the most common unadmitted fantasies among human males—and I understand perfectly well why! A three-forked tongue under complete voluntary control; a mouth without teeth, with rotating chewing plates of cartilage, not bone, in their place... It's a little like sublimating the great masculine nightmare of the vagina dentata.

But what do you want? Maybe I'm old-school, but for me that sort of contact will never take the place of "the thing itself."

Oral sex—like written sex—will never be anything but tender foreplay or a pathetic emergency substitute for real intercourse. Accept no substitutes. Forget about it. Sorry, but that's how it is.

Calling each other milk cousins means that my former employee and Gardf here both ingested the nutritious "milk" that induced their metamorphosis into humanoids from the same male. Or at least think they did, for many experts still heatedly debate whether adults have any memory of their larval stage.

It goes without saying that this common experience unites Cetian society, which is obviously matriarchal and has nothing remotely like sexual dynamics (no, by all indications they are *not* a culture of rabidly lusty lesbians, as perversely attractive as the possibility may appear to a few hotheaded humans), by forming much more intimate clans than human consanguinity could ever create.

*

"Umm... Perdón about the mixup. So, cómo está An-Mhaly?" I finally manage to ask her silver-skirted twin, overcoming my natural initial embarrassment and the torrent of thoughts and memories that her words have unleashed in me.

The Galactic Community Coordinating Committee official flashes her huge yellow eyes at me in a way I've never seen any of her fellow Cetians do, but I can tell she's signifying deep disapproval. At last she says with a sigh, "I won't lie to you, Doctor Sangan. An está in bad shape. She'll never get over tu... rejection. Su case is very talked-about en Tau Ceti."

"Perdón," I say, because I can't say anything else. I say it with all my heart, though, I swear. "She was una asistente magnífica and an even better secretaria. Pero you have to entender, given our anatomical diferencias..."

"I do entiendo." Gardf-Mhaly gives me another one of those stone-cold looks. "Though in el pasado that hasn't stopped otros hombres from at least trying to consumar their amor imposible... Anyway, ella también entiende that you'd never have been able to join completamente, hablando físicamente. But el amor—don't we know it bien!—goes beyond lo físico, even lo químico. Far beyond." Her ears fold back, a sign of barely controlled rage. "Doctor Sangan, conoce usted the terrestrial myth of the mermaids? Surely que si. Half-mujer, half-pez, they attracted hombres and then los frustraron porque they were anatómicamente incapable of mating, being fish that fertilized externamente. Debió have been hard en los hombres, I guess. But did los hombres ever wonder cómo se sentían las mermaids? Yo creo que An-Mhaly could explain it perfectamente well..."

When they go for it, Cetians can shock even extreme feminists, making them look moderate and wishy-washy by contrast.

Though there's no consummation, of course, one might suppose, or rather deduce, that within their clans they practice a certain very light and sublimated version of homoerotic sex—an idea that many XY humans, easily carried away by their imaginations, find attractive, even fascinating.

I guess the guys who only know a little about the species must imagine something like hundreds of beautiful, exotic girls caressing each other for hours and hours, gently and absent-mindedly, all of them piled up all over each other...

Maybe that's how it really is. Or not. They don't divulge any details, of course. And that's their right, despite all the grumbling among interspecies medical experts that without more information, they'll never be able to treat their traumas...

But I wonder if this Cetian (An's occasional lover? her casual caresser?) isn't simply dying of jealousy to think I aroused feelings in her unlucky milk cousin, feelings better saved for members of her own race—such as herself.

Or am I perhaps acting out the worst form of narcissistic machismo... Sangan Dongo, the irresistible supermacho of the Milky Way?

I hold my tongue for a couple of seconds, then repeat with sincere contrition, "De verdad que I am sorry. Yo nunca thought she'd take it tan badly."

"Doctor Sangan, no tenemos doctores of the mind, lo que usted llama psychologists," Gardf-Mhaly went on, looking down on me as the haughtiest queen might look upon the least tadpole in her pond. "We've never needed them... Pero with An we ahora believe we probablemente have to resort to uno for la primera vez. There have been a few... situaciones... en el pasado, of course, but su caso caused us to cuestionar whether the Arnrch-Morp-Gulch entailment isn't a curse for nuestra raza rather than para el progreso. Perhaps no estamos and never will be listos to deal with una comunidad of intelligent species que all display algo we lack: intercourse heterosexual. Muchos de nosotros find it... perverso. I believe you may be familiar con la sensación. But there are siempre those such as the unlucky An que look upon such... uniones with wonder y envidia, leading to the tristes consequences of which estamos both aware." She sighs, then unfurls her ears again in an obvious effort to appear friendly. "Pero I did not venir aquí looking for a debate sobre interspecies sexual relations, Doctor Sangan, solamente para your asistencia urgente. This is su chance to correct past errores. An-Mhaly needs you—as does otros former employee of yours, Enti Kmusa. Both have been perdidos in a small exploration vessel..."

"No way, esos dos together again?" I interrupt her, astonished. "Quién would have thought! It's a cosmos pequeño, o no? I understand por qué I've been contacted, since both of them used to trabajar para mí. But if it's sobre un shipwreck, that's de verdad something for the local Galactic Community Coordinating Committee patrols, no para mí to take care..."

"No, Doctor Sangan," Gardf-Mhaly peremptorily insisted. "There is no one major que you. Ellos están indeed shipwrecked.

And ellos necesitan be rescued as rápido as possible, porque they nunca should have crashed—or rather, their crash is such a secreto que nadie can even be allowed to sospechar que it took place. Pero the fact es, the ship on which An-Mhaly and Enti Kmusa were viajando has fallen in Brobdingnag..."

*

Quite the coincidence.

With or without permission from Jonathan Swift and his Gulliver, Brobdingnag is the world where laketons live.

I first heard about the creatures when I was eight.

I was with my father on one of his typical expeditions, this time to study the peculiar hypnopedic teaching system used by a religious sect on Beta Sextantis.

The deluded people there had concocted an intricate theology rooted in the worst aspects of New Age ecomysticism; they worshiped living beings, the bigger the better, as organic expressions of the Great Cosmic Principle.

More recently I've worked for them, on several occasions, actually. Their faith may be ridiculous, but they pay well and on time.

Even back then, their temple-zoo, which cost I don't even want to know how many millions of solaria to build, held a grendel, two juggernauts, and, in a tank big enough for a squadron of battleships to perform maneuvers in, a middling-sized tsunami... They were also building an enormous high-pressure enclosure with the idea of keeping a laketon, no less! An idea that made Dr. Matsumoto Sangan and his entire team laugh till they cried.

When I asked my father what a laketon was, he gave me an unforgettable mini lecture on biology that might well have been titled "Las características del Planet Brobdingnag y de sus Inhabitants los Laketons, the Largest Life Form en el Known Universe, Explaneado para Children," and he got me to understand why he had laughed at the pretensions of those environmentalist mystics.

Brobdingnag is the only planet orbiting its primary star, a red dwarf. The star can't be seen from Earth, being hidden precisely behind the supergiant Antares. Therefore ancient human astronomers never gave it a name. Even today many know it only as Swift-3.

Swift-3 is located in a zone rich in cosmic dust, comet formations, and protoplanets. Head towards the Juhungan domain until you figure out you can't breathe the hydrogen there, then zoom past the Amphorians, where you can check to see if methane works any better for you, and at last you'll reach the edge of the Cetian sector, where you can enjoy the oxygen you needed all along.

The primary star is small, but the planet is enormous, just a tad smaller than Neptune in humanity's original solar system. As big as a planet can get before being categorized as a true gas giant. It even looks quite a bit like the gas giants: though it's completely solid, it has four or five dozen satellites and several tenuous rings, like Jupiter, Saturn, and Uranus.

Since the planet lacks a dense metallic core and is composed of fairly porous material, the gravity at its surface is "only" six times that on Earth—not past the limits of human resistance. We're forced to withstand many more *g*'s than that on plenty of shuttle launches and descents from orbit... But it's a very uncomfortable place to stay for any length of time. That's why almost everyone prefers to use space elevators to enter or leave a planet, except when they are truly pressed for time—as I was when Governor Tarkon called me to search for his careless spouse's damned wedding band...

The massive gravitational force of Brobdingnag, plus the fact that it's the only planet orbiting a small primary in a sector full of dust, comets, and other space trash, means that its surface is constantly pounded by heavy meteor showers. The meteoroids that reach its surface usually weigh a few kilos, but more than a few have masses ranging from hundreds of kilograms to a ton or more.

The crew of the *Fancy Appaloosa*, the human exploratory ship out of New Plymouth that discovered Swift-3 and mapped Brobdingnag right under the Cetians' noses, the system being much closer to the Cetian sphere of influence than to ours, named the planet less for its own size (much larger planets exist) than for the vast dimensions of its principle inhabitants: the laketons, for which this rain of cosmic debris is a sort of manna from heaven.

The astronauts got a real shock when they realized, gazing through their telescopes from orbit, that what they initially thought were large chemical lakes scattered across the giant planet's desolate surface were... slowly moving.

Laketons are unicellular amoeboid creatures. Since their form constantly changes, it isn't easy to determine their exact dimensions.

But they're big.

In fact, all adjectives seem miserably small and inadequate to describe them.

One fact should be enough to convey their vastness: The largest laketon ever recorded, which the veterinarian biologists who study them sarcastically and affectionately named Tiny, rarely measures less than 250 kilometers (!) in diameter by 10 kilometers thick.

If its cytoplasm were the density of water, it would weigh approximately *250 trillion tons*. On Earth, that is. Given the gravity on Brobdingnag, you have to multiply that by six.

But actually, the protoplasm of a laketon is even denser than liquid mercury, which already weighs more than thirteen times as much as water.

I think that adds up to some *twenty quadrillion tons*. There are moons that weigh less.

Living *lakes* weighing trillions of *tons*. Laketons.

Just trying to imagine them is overwhelming.

And sort of humbling, too.

There's no ship, no building, no artificial structure of any sort built by humans or any of the other "happy seven" intelligent races in the Milky Way that come close to their dimensions. Experts even think that the individual movements of a single laketon can cause minor fluctuations in the gravity of Brobdingnag and explain some curious irregularities in its orbit around Swift-3 that would have disconcerted Kepler.

And no one knows the upper limit on a laketon's growth, if it has one. As living matter, it keeps growing larger and larger, slowly but surely. Tiny has grown a bit and put on some weight over the thirty-four years since the species was discovered. Today it's about two hundred meters wider and half a trillion tons heavier than before.

Since its smallest fellow laketons, Gargantua and Pantagruel, are "merely" sixty kilometers in diameter and grow at a proportionately slower rate, experts have concluded that Tiny has been the largest cell and living creature in the galaxy since long before humans discovered fire.

A peevish Parimazo once calculated that at its current rate of growth, in about six billion years Tiny would outweigh all of Brobdingnag and might even be larger than its primary star, Swift-3. And in three and a half billion years, it could outweigh the combined mass of the Milky Way.

It's good to know we won't be around by then. Just in case.

Naturally, not even a planet as huge as Brobdingnag can harbor many creatures as immense as laketons. Only 611 of them have been counted moving across its surface.

The "small" laketons, Gargantua and Pantagruel, are assumed to be mere cubs. As weird as it seems to use the word "cubs" for those monstrosities, which must have been born around the time Columbus was discovering America, at the latest.

The speculation is that laketons reproduce by simple binary fission, like many well-known protozoa, but to date the process has never been witnessed. Given their longevity, whole centuries might pass before one decides to start dividing. The event might depend on some planetary alignment, or a cellular clock set by an unusually long biological time scale... or who knows what else. So much is still unknown about laketons.

The titanic amoeba of Brobdingnag has a feeding method as spectacular as its size. It has no eyes or ears, and it wouldn't even need them to capture its "prey": the meteoroids continuously falling from space. Its cellular membrane, several meters thick in some areas, is highly resistant to cosmic and ultraviolet rays but also extremely sensitive to changes in the intensity of light, air pressure, and, above all, gravity.

No gravimeter made by humans or any of the other "lucky seven" races could compete. A laketon has been shown to have the ability to detect a fragment with a mass of only ten kilos falling through the planet's atmosphere at a distance unimaginable for any artificial instrument. By some unknown means, which must be entirely instinctive given that it has nothing remotely resembling a brain, it instantly completes the complex ballistic calculations that reveal the meteoroid's velocity and trajectory, telling it to a very close approximation where its delicious "snack" will fall—and allowing it to capture the meteor in flight.

A laketon can also determine—by spectrography, long-distance taste, smell, or some other poorly understood sense—whether the meteoroid is an indigestible fragment of purely inorganic rock with metallic ore (best avoided) or a succulent cometary agglomeration of ice water or carbonaceous chondrites (not to be missed).

It also has a sense of its own reach and abilities that would make it the envy of many baseball players. If the impact site is too far off, it doesn't even budge, but if the zone lies instead at a reasonable distance, it will stretch trillions of tons of cytoplasm in that direction at the speed of an express train, forming a pseudopod dozens of kilometers long by a few hundred meters wide, which it uses to capture the meteoroid before it touches the ground.

Fly ball! Yer out.

How it absorbs the tremendous kinetic energy of the impact, dissipating it throughout its gigantic body without the heat generated by the blow vaporizing its cytoplasm or causing any other damage, is an enigma that has fascinated engineers and biologists alike. But so far, in vain.

A pity, because you could perform miracles with a thermal conduction system as efficient as that.

Engineers also dream of constructing similar gravitational wave detectors and/or controls for spaceships. Biologists, for their part, fantasize about synthesizing materials to keep astronauts equally comfortable in weightlessness or under dozens of g's of acceleration.

While they're at it, they'd love to discover the genetic mechanisms behind these creatures' unmatched longevity.

It is a law of biology that the more massive an animal is, the longer it lives. Tsunamis and other giants tend to be quite long-lived. But even titans die.

So far, no laketon has ever been known to die. Some biologists even doubt they can. It's hard to imagine the sort of planetary cataclysm it would take to wipe out so much living matter.

In short, they're fascinating bugs. Given their huge size and the powerful gravity on their home world, they are studied from the comfort of orbit, using telescopes. Floating in weightlessness while observing such magnificent beings can be an absorbing occupation—but also monotonous and boring; no observer can take it for more than a week.

But of course there's never any shortage of enthusiastic volunteers to take their place. The crew of the *Fancy Appaloosa* would have been surprised to learn that four fully crewed biological observation ships are now in permanent orbit around the planet that they somewhat rashly described as being "of no interest whatsoever." Each ship holds four observers... and the waitlist holds the names of more than fifteen thousand applicants, with representatives from each of the "lucky seven" races.

Mine is one of them. I checked my place on the *loooong* list a few days before Governor Tarkon called me to Nerea, and there were still three thousand applicants ahead of me, so I'd have to wait "only" another three and a half years...

They're popular critters, no doubt about it. At least among veterinarian biologists like me.

My never having been within fifty light-years of a laketon was a painful, unpardonable gap in my résumé. What sort of a "Veterinarian to the Giants" was I, if I hadn't been able to study the largest of all known living beings?

Aside from two or three parasites, which some even doubt count as distinct and independent species, there seem to be no life forms on Brobdingnag other than laketons. So it wasn't strange at all for me to volunteer, without a moment's hesitation, the second I deduced from what Gardf-Mhaly was saying that the affair would involve the titans I had yearned to see for so long.

There's an old Cuban saying: "If he doesn't want soup, give him three bowlfuls."

But what if he does want soup? What then? Pelt him with bouillon cubes?

*

To lend a little stylistic variety to my still-pending autobiography (and who knows how much longer it will pend), I could narrate my face-to-face meeting with Gardf-Mhaly and the other top brass in the Galactic Community Coordinating Committee in the form of a play.

Might be interesting.

It would go something like this:

SCENE: *Inside a Juhungan mother ship. Probably a hangar for faster, smaller attack craft, judging from its size and the honeycombed walls. In this room, the volutes of germanium polymerase foam that characterize the hydrogen breathers' organic constructs are lined with a neutral boron nitride coating, allowing the beings engaged in heated debate around a giant holoprojection to breathe oxygen freely without danger of compromising the vehicle's internal structure.*

There are two Cetians, two humans, and one Juhungan. The last, barely a meter tall, is apparently the host; he only watches, takes no part. Decked out in an organic spacesuit typical of his species, he looks like a gigantic, transparent sea urchin.

The members of the two oxygen-breathing races, wearing a variety of uniforms all tinted the distinctive silver of the Galactic Community Coordinating Committee, argue among themselves in Spanglish.

GARDF-MHALY, CETIAN COORDINATOR: Este ship acaba de docked; he'll be aquí in a few minutos. Insisto que we must tell him toda la verdad. The fact que sus two former employees happened to coincide en estos... discussions may be a signo. The Goddess esta trying to tell us algo...

ADMIRAL WILLIAM HURTADO, HUMAN COORDINATOR: Yes, que we've got a ticking bomba de tiempo en our hands! Goddess o no Goddess, if young Kmusa no regresa a home within las próximas seventy-two horas, the gang of Olduvailan fanatics que follow her como they used to follow a su padre will pensar que she fell into a Cetian trap. They'll atacar, y luego you can kiss adiós a nuestro ceasefire y to any hopes of settling nuestras interspecies differences pacíficamente.

CONFLICTMASTER JHUN-LIKHA, CETIAN COORDINATOR: Admiral, does it not le preocupa what my people might hacer if they creen their envoy fue asesinado by the human colonizers ilegales? Su frustrated and regrettable… romantic affair con the human Sangan Dongo has made her muy popular among our people. If she does not regresa soon, ni siquiera nosotros, their elected military leaders, will be able to controlar la situación. The anti-human faction es already very strong, and if they come al poder, an immediate escalation de ataques on the Olduvailans will follow.

GENERAL JUNICHIRO KURCHATOV, HUMAN COORDINATOR: Let's hope que no llegue to that. No, en honor a la memoria of the fallen of both our razas at the Second Battle of Canaan… But quite right, no estamos as worried sobre what your people may do pero sobre how these rebellious colonizers might reaccionar. Probablemente porque we are confidentes that you will transmitir nuestras más sincere apologies a your people—and that they'll be un poco más rationales than we humans tend to be en such cases… y will accept them.

GARDF-MHALY: It is sad for un líder to place más trust in the equanimity of sus rivales than in that of the members de su propia race.

WILLIAM HURTADO: Probablemente it's sad, pero it's también very realístico. Besides, nosotros no somos rivales. Not ahora, anyway... Pero I insist in any case that Doctor Sangan should be given as little información as possible. Él es just un civilian. And the truth is, you've already told him demasiado.

At this point, realizing that the tense atmosphere could precipitate a genuine confrontation, the Juhungan observer-host speaks up, even though he isn't a Coordinator and is theoretically outranked by everyone else in the room.

Let's call him Mkron-Rve. Human and Cetian lips and throats would be completely incapable of pronouncing his actual name, of course.

Mkron-Rve activates the symbiotic translator-telepath that he wears attached to two of the spines on his uniform. The small organism, which looks somewhat like a quadruped parrot with feather-like antennae, instantly puts his thought-ideas into words.

In proper Spanglish, he basically says that neither the human race nor the Cetians will last much longer unless they both take extreme measures and, most importantly, move quickly. But they are rather foolishly letting their arguments get in the way of that goal.

Then Mkron-Rve adds, speaking of course through the translator-symbiote, that the Olduvailan humans illegally occupying Cetian territory are also civilians, and in any case, everyone present here must not forget that they are on board a combat vessel put at their disposal by the Most Correct Hegemony of Juhung in a manifest sign of goodwill, as representatives of two companion races of the Galactic Community, in order that they may resolve their problems with no further violence—something that the highest governing body of the right honorable hydrogen-breathing race would never have done without first completing an exhaustive study of the most obscure details of the situation.

Juhung, according to some experts, means "la people que use all las words correctamente."

Emphasis on all…

JHUN-LIKHA: Mkron-Rve habla wisely. Él deserves to be made un Coordinator. No tenemos tiempo for debating detalles or assigning blame; debemos forget nuestras diferencias and undertake un joint rescue. As for data leaks… bear en mente que Doctor Sangan might have refused to take on el caso si two of his former employees were not envueltas. That was algo we could not risk. On my planet nosotros decimos, "Discover dónde están el honor y también duty y the people will follow."

JUNICHIRO KURCHATOV: Well, on Earth nosotros decimos, "Discover dónde están los profits y people will come corriendo." Given the laketons, yo creo que this Sangan should have rushed aquí on the double even if su peor enemigo were involved. He's been trying to get cerca to them por años. I've been following su carrera for a long tiempo; él tiene the skills, for sure, pero he wasn't un especially brilliant estudiante at Anima Mundi, did you know?

MHALY: You have been keeping un ojo en him for so long, General? I think that data point alone suffices para mostrar how special él es. My milk cousin An-Mhaly once harbored, and probablemente still harbors, strong feelings por this Sangan. Therefore I thought him deserving de la verdad. He is a good person. For a human and an hombre, that is.

HURTADO: Okay, maybe we're judging al hombre too harshly. For a Cetian to fall in love con él, he must not be your run-of-the-mill personaje. Nosotros don't have a whole lot of otras opciones, either. Let's let him try the rescue—so long as he signs the most ironclad, restrictive secret confidentiality agreement que nuestros abogados can produce before he lands on Brobdingnag.

LIKHA: As you quiera. Yo insisto that having him work without knowing todos los detalles is más dangerous, not safer. And we truly tenemos few alternativas.

KURCHATOV: So it's agreed. Tres a uno. For the record, yo estoy en contra, pero... majority rules. Send him in.

And this is where I walk in.

Alone, of course, because when it comes to confidentiality you're better off not counting on Narbuk. Oh, he'll keep a lid on it, alright, but he'll bang that lid like a kettledrum. The Laggoru's brain is an echo chamber: He's genetically incapable of keeping things to himself. The second you tell the reptilian a secret, it ceases to be a secret.

So, ignoring his protests, I've sent him on to Abyssalia, non-stop. And on his own. Let him figure things out for himself without hiding in my shadow for once. Maybe he can resolve the problem of the grendels spawning out of season without having to get close to them, maybe not. In either case, he's such a virtuoso at making up excuses, he might be able to convince the anxious ecologists that I'm late getting to them because I've run into unavoidable obstacles.

I'm also a bit confused, I won't deny it. Because the ultrarapid shuttlecraft that Gardf-Mhaly hired for me hasn't exactly brought me to Brobdingnag...

But rather to something orbiting it. My first impression was that it looked like the enormous excrement of some unknown space organism—not a pleasant thought at all, just a few hours after the tsunami business on Nerea, which gave me enough scatology lessons to last three lifetimes. But when I entered the object, I could see it was a non-human space vehicle.

Indescribable from the outside, it didn't look Cetian or Laggoru from the inside, either.

What, then? Amphorian? Parimazo? Kerkant?

Or maybe... Juhungan?

What would the hydrogen breathers be doing in the middle of this spat between two oxygen-breathing species? Why so much fuss about rescuing a couple of my old assistants?

To cap it all off, as soon as I walked in I recognized Kurchatov. Of course, that's not the name that first came to mind.

Because, as it turns out, this hardass big shot used to be a bit of a slacker when he studied two years of veterinarian biology with me at Anna Mundi...

Back then he was a party animal, famous for getting soused every night. Our friendly nickname for him was Juni Tacho.

Obviously, this was before three generations of scientists in his family finally accepted the fact that he was only interested in colonial insects because his real calling was in the military—something they had obstinately refused to consider possible before then.

Pity about the kid. He was pretty obsessed with soldier ants, militaristic beetles, and the like, but he could have made a good veterinarian biologist. We missed him a lot in our "oceanography studies" over the next few semesters. I was the only one who could out-drink him, and not by many teaspoons...

And now here he is, a full-blown general with so much gold braid on his shoulders it's a wonder he can hold them up. I hope, for his subordinates' sake, he doesn't still drink C_2H_5OH compounds as enthusiastically as he did when he was a student...

Living proof of the miraculous memory-scrubbing effects of high rank, my former classmate shows no sign of recognizing me—so instead of invoking our old Anima Mundian alcoholical familiarities, I keep my mouth respectfully shut.

A prudent attitude when faced with so much power gathered in so few square meters, I think.

ME: Umm... Hola, Gardf-Mhaly, delighted to meet you en persona, I mean, close up. (I register Hurtado's rank, realize that Kurchatov has the equivalent rank in the Army of Earth, that they all work for the Coordinating Committee, and I gulp; now I really start to worry.) Admiral? General? Our Cetian friend me dijo que el accidente de Enti y An-Mhaly era un secreto, pero...

HURTADO AND KURCHATOV (*in chorus*): We aren't aquí. Nosotros never gave you la misión que estamos about to entrust you with. If you succeed, nadie will ever know, y there will be no medallas. If you fail... la culpa will be yours alone.

ME: Okay; voy a necesitar the smallest, sturdiest ship you've got. Not a bioship, por favor: a traditional design, human si es posible, good solid metal y plástico. With superpowerful ion máquinas, a magnetohydrodynamic propulsion system, room aboard para tres personas, y a g-force cushioning system. También, at least six motherships with powerful engines, preferiblemente human Tornado-class frigate carriers; unos five hundred kilómetros de carbón nanotube fiber cable; seis toneladas de table salt; dos toneladas de colchicine o algún toxic secondary metabolite similar; y...

LIKHA (*interrupting me*): Doctor Sangan, do these specific requests significan que you have already mastered todos los detalles de la situación?

ME (*arrogantly*): What's there to master? Enti y An-Mhaly took a trip para recordar about old times, they got muy cerca de

Brobdingnag, they got caught by the planet's tremendous gravedad, they came tumbling out of el cielo, y luego a lake-ton mistook them for comida and encased them in one of its alimentary vacuoles. Since those mega-amoebas no pueden digerir inorganic matter, en un par de semanas a lo mucho the bug will expel them, after the digestive vacuole encasing them los convierta en excretory organelle. So yo supongo que ellos no deben tener mucho oxygen left, or there wouldn't be all this urgencia.

HURTADO AND KURCHATOV *(in chorus)*: Eso es exactly what happened. Muy astute, Doctor Sangan. Give us su shopping list y we'll get it all para usted on the double so you can get moving lo antes posible.

MHALY: Yes, it is an urgent case, muy urgente. Pero no por falta de oxygen. It is that... Enti Kmusa y An-Mhaly did not exactly pass by Brobdingnag por accidente, and things did not go precisamente as you suggested, Doctor Sangan.

ME: Entonces, tell me how it really went down, as accurately as you pueda...

This calls for a shift to a more schematic, data-based style so I can skip the endless tug-of-war it took for me to drag a precise idea of the matter from the teeth of their military penchant for secrecy.

For example, I could express it all in syllogisms, so Argol Swendal, my symbolic-logic professor at Anima Mundi, might feel proud of me at least this once:

FIRST SYLLOGISM

FIRST PREMISE: Garden planet with oxygen atmosphere, relatively nonaggressive fauna, and exuberant flora, third from a type G2 yellow dwarf star; that is, very similar to the humans' Sun. A tempting nugget for any colony scheme.

SECOND PREMISE: Planetary system on the border between the human and Cetian zones. Humans name the promising planet Canaan. Cetians call it Urgh-Yhaly-Mhan, which in the language of the Goddess means "we deserve this because we are who we are."

THIRD PREMISE: Both species are highly expansionistic and will not hesitate to turn to violence if they think it necessary to support and/or safeguard their interests.

CONCLUSION: To avoid sparking a large-scale armed conflict, in the years following the First Battle of Canaan (a minor skirmish that left thousands of casualties on both sides) neither race risks settling the tempting border world. They sign a solemn treaty sanctioning this unstable but reassuring equilibrium. A tiny joint garrison of troops from both species will oversee compliance.

SECOND SYLLOGISM

FIRST PREMISE: Far, far from Canaan, the grassland planet Olduvaila, a First Wave human colony world, has barely eight-tenths the gravity of Earth. Its inhabitants, descendants of the Maasai people, average seven feet in height as adults and specialize in cattle ranching.

SECOND PREMISE: Bwana, a gas giant approximately the size of Saturn and the fourth planet in the same system, passes near Olduvaila every fourteen years, and with each pass it overwhelms the colonial world's weaker gravity and captures a bit more of its atmosphere. This process has been going on for millions of years... but after two or three more passes, the declining density of the local atmosphere will leave it too thin for the humans and their herds to breathe. Already the air on Olduvaila is barely equivalent to the atmosphere at an altitude of five thousand meters on Earth.

THIRD PREMISE: The Maasai, a cattle-herding African people from whom the human colonizers on Olduvaila are descended, have a strong warrior tradition and have never resigned themselves to being defeated by drought, famine, other natural disasters... or any enemy.

CONCLUSION: The warlike and desperate inhabitants of the dying planet Olduvaila are seeking another world where they can move. Urgently and en masse, no matter where it is and no matter whose bodies they have to step over to get there.

THIRD SYLLOGISM

FIRST PREMISE: One fine day, 3,600 ships appear unannounced at Urgh-Yhaly-Mhan, or Canaan to the humans.

Their crews total more than sixty thousand well-armed people who are ready for anything: the advance guard of the Olduvailan migration. They are led by the old and skillful populist politician Mvamba Kmusa.

SECOND PREMISE: Grown lax after three long decades of peace following the First Battle of Canaan, the minuscule joint human-Cetian garrison is taken completely by surprise. But in an unforgettable show of interracial cooperation, the human members of the force, including two soldiers from Olduvaila, fight as fiercely as the Cetians against the much larger invading forces, delaying their landing for as long as they can... until the last soldier falls.

THIRD PREMISE: During the bitterly fought Second Battle of Canaan, a costly Pyrrhic victory for the invading forces, old Mvamba dies. By Olduvailan political tradition, power passes to his daughter, Enti Kmusa. But the heroic resistance of the mixed human-Cetian garrison bought enough time to prevent the expeditionary force from completing its mission of clearing the way for the rest of the colonizers to land. The entire Cetian fleet rushes to blockade the illegally occupied planet, preventing reinforcements from joining the Olduvailan advance guard occupying the ground.

CONCLUSION: An old tactical axiom states that it is impossible to use an attack from space, even by overwhelmingly superior forces, to dislodge any planetary position that has been reinforced with nuclear artillery and missiles—which Enti Kmusa and her followers possess in abundance. As the colonizers cannot be expelled from Canaan (which they immediately renamed New Olduvaila) or receive reinforcements from the rest of their people, the situation has frozen into an exasperating impasse that has gone on for six years now—though for once, the Galactic Community Coordinating Committee has managed to keep a pretty tight lid on it.

FOURTH SYLLOGISM

FIRST PREMISE: The leadership of the Olduvailan rebels, watching their supplies and ammunition dwindle, realize that their position is militarily and politically untenable. Yet the morale of their troops is as high as on the first day, and they won't hear a word about surrender, treaties, or concessions. They've conquered a new homeland, and they have no intention of relinquishing New Olduvaila.

SECOND PREMISE. The Cetians, feeling affronted, demand that the human race expel the intruders unconditionally from Urgh-Yhaly-Mhan... or exterminate them. But their military leaders would prefer to come to an agreement with the illegal occupiers. They feel that, in the name of peace, they could grant them a consolation prize—some other world, one not quite so heavenly as Canaan or (preferably) so close to Tau Ceti.

THIRD PREMISE: The governments of the other five races in the Galactic Community are prepared to do everything possible to bring the warring factions to an understanding.

CONCLUSION: The Most Correct Juhungan Hegemony assault ship *Imperturbable Eviscerator of Unredeemed Suns* (or something of the sort; translations from the Juhungan can never be exact) offers the use of its facilities to the two contending parties while they negotiate a treaty. In absolute secrecy.

FIFTH SYLLOGISM

FIRST PREMISE: Taking the Cetian side in the discussions is Coordinator Gardf-Mhaly's honorable milk cousin, An-Mhaly, whose impossible love for a stonyhearted human (the author of these lines) has made her a romantic heroine among her people. Her one-time friendship with the current leader of New Olduvaila, who worked as an assistant for the same human, will, it is hoped, facilitate their negotiation of a just treaty that neither side will find too dishonorable.

SECOND PREMISE: Given Enti Kmusa's paranoid fear that even the giant Juhungan warship isn't safe from prying eyes and ears, the patient hydrogen breathers offer her and the Cetian one of their many secondary vehicles so that, while traveling an undisclosed route, they can have all the time and secrecy they desire to nail down the details of the pact.

THIRD PREMISE: The small exploration vessel in question is organic, like all Juhungan technology. Carbon-reinforced germanium foam. And it flies dangerously close to Brobdingnag.

CONCLUSION: When their vehicle is captured by the gigantic planet's gravitational field, the Cetian negotiator and the leader of the illegal occupiers of New Olduvai/Canaan/Urgh-Yhaly-Mhan cannot prevent it from plummeting to the planet's surface—where a laketon, attracted by the irresistibly delicious chemical composition of the Juhungan vehicle, promptly devours it.

SIXTH SYLLOGISM

FIRST PREMISE: Enti Kmusa and An-Mhaly must be freed as quickly and as secretly as possible so the conflict between Olduvailans and Cetians doesn't flare up and drag on forever.

SECOND PREMISE: The laketon that "kidnapped" them is none other than the second largest of the 611 inhabiting the planet, after Tiny. Called Cosita, it is nearly two hundred kilometers wide. They have to be rescued right away, before the chemical contents of the digestive vacuole completely dissolve and assimilate the organic Juhungan ship—along with its two passengers.

THIRD PREMISE: Given its extremely thick cellular wall and its natural resistance to radiation and impacts, any weapon powerful enough to cause discernible damage to Cosita is just as likely to annihilate its precious "prisoners" in the process. CONCLUSION: What they need is a miracle rescue. What they need is Jan Amos Sangan Dongo, a.k.a. the "Veterinarian to the Giants." He's said to be amazing, surprising, a genius (viewed objectively). If he can't extract them from the laketon's innards, nobody can. And besides—what a coincidence!—it turns out he's well acquainted with the "kidnapping victims," so they'll trust him.

And if he succeeds... he'll get paid a prize of... would ten million solaria be okay?

Or maybe, since I'm such a surprising, amazing genius, I should ask for a little more?

*

That, basically, was how my secret meeting went with the Head Honchos of Operation Negotiator Rescue.

End result of the interview?

They convinced me. Though I was already set to go before we started.

As a consequence, here I am, stuck in this ship and barely able to squirm, what with the hydraulic bucket seat, the g-force cushioning capsule, and all the extra equipment I stashed on board.

Lots of weight. As if it weren't enough to be carrying a regulation complement of God-knows-how-many missiles, which the sarcastic Kurchatov insisted they didn't have time to unload from the magazines. Typical top-brass bureaucrat brain... Or maybe he's holding on to his trump card, the ability to destroy me by remote control if anything goes wrong?

Deal with the military and...

I'm starting to sound paranoid...

Which doesn't mean they aren't really out to get me, you know.

But in any case, I'll have to dump all this ballast before returning to orbit or there won't be room in the cabin for the pair I'm rescuing. Besides, the engines couldn't take the added weight.

I insisted on using a human vehicle on my exotic mission, not a Juhungan ship. It's more familiar—and all metal and glass, with nothing organic to whet a laketon's appetite, not even if the bug is starving.

And they humored me.

I took command of this three-seater, with its military design and atmospheric aerodynamics (can't divulge any more details; still top-secret) and christened it *Beagle* after the ship on which Darwin circumnavigated Earth back in his day, when he was still working on the theory of natural selection that would make him immortal.

I hope the little homage will bring me luck. I'll need it, and how.

I'm hoping to show certain people a few things.

Show Enti Kmusa and An-Mhaly that I bear them no ill will. And that I always appreciated them...

Though, as I've finally realized, I was just too shy to make sexual advances.

Well, if I rescue them, maybe we'll get a second chance.

I seriously need to rethink mixing business with pleasure...

My father, who has the most flexible morals ever, always says there's nothing wrong with having strict principles, so long as they don't lead you astray.

And since I've heard so many interesting things lately about how Cetians give incredible head...

I also want to show all the military types—really want to rub in their big fat faces (or the anatomical equivalent thereof, whether human, Cetian, or Juhungan)—that I can keep a secret, too, even if I am a civilian. And that calling myself the "Veterinarian to the Giants" is more than a cheap publicity slogan and empty bragging; it's a title I earned the hard way, case after case.

I'm especially determined to make that fact crystal-clear to a certain contemptuous reformed alcoholic and former classmate of mine from Anima Mundi who's now a puffed-up general in the Army of Earth and acting like he'd really love to see me fail...

I'll never understand why some people find it so hard to recognize a drop of talent or ability in people they were once pretty close to. I imagine Jesus of Nazareth's neighbors used to say dismissively, "Turn water into wine? Joe the carpenter's kid? C'mon, you gotta be kidding! When that brat was little he played in the mud down at the creek in front of my house, just like all the others!"

As for Cosita, the second largest cell in the galaxy...

Truth be told, I hope it never finds out I exist.

I'm so modest, aren't I?

Well, this job won't be easy, but as Jack the Ripper would say, let's take it one piece at a time.

First step in any rescue is getting to where the captives are being held.

Which mean getting to Cosita, on the surface of Brobdingnag. Easier said than done.

Understatement of the year.

The number one obstacle to exploring the surface of a giant planet is its monstrous gravity, of course. Just landing on and taking off from the surface of an Earth-sized world subjects you to accelerations several times normal gravity. Only young, resilient, and very fit bodies can take it without getting hurt.

And that's not me today, if it ever was. I don't have to look in a mirror to know it.

Up until now this has never gotten much in my way. If the González drive opened a doorway to the stars, space elevators have been almost as important. They brought the doorway down from the twentieth floor—too high for old folks and non-athletic types, who otherwise would still be stuck up there—and put it at ground level.

"Orbital elevators—the cosmos for everyone," went one optimistic twenty-first-century ad.

Trying to land on a world like Brobdingnag in a shuttle with ion-propulsion engines would multiply its already exasperating gravity, six times that of Earth, by a factor of seven or eight. And I don't have the slightest intention of getting my bones pulverized, not by forty-two g's, and not by forty-eight.

For all the difference it makes...

On the other hand, it would take weeks and weeks, at a bare minimum, to build an orbital elevator.

That's time we don't have.

So after racking my brains for a few minutes, I came up with a way to jerry-rig an emergency space elevator.

Am I or am I not a "surprising, amazing genius"?

Get thee behind me, modesty!

Now, some things turn out to be quite easy. When they give you carte blanche to use practically all the resources of the Galactic Community Coordinating Committee, that is.

Not six, but eight mother ships have been placed at my disposal. Not exactly human Tornado-class frigate carriers (Hurtado prudently noted that he would just as soon let the army under his command learn as little as possible about the matter) but their Juhungan equivalents: *Indisputable Glory to the Most Correct Hegemony*-class forward command posts. A little larger, but with slightly less powerful engines. Thus, eight instead of six.

Assembled, the titanic octet formed the orbital anchor point from which I began my descent in my *Beagle*, dangling like a spider from its thread: five hundred kilometers of carbon nano-tube cables, made rigid by piezoelectric effect as it unspooled.

Standard orbital elevators are made of the same material. The difference is that elevators are normally designed to carry a huge volume of traffic weighing much more than my light *Beagle*, so the cables used on the most densely populated planets are four, even five meters thick.

Whereas I'm clinging to a cable barely ten centimeters in diameter. Basically a single hair, thin and light. The five hundred kilometers equal a little under five hundred tons. A weight that my eight Juhungan plow mules can handle with relative ease, though only if they all pull together with their ionic engines.

The crew of the *Fancy Appaloosa*, who had to make do with viewing the surface of the planet they discovered from orbit, would have died of envy if they had seen this.

Descending to a planet's surface by elevator is easy, but mind you, nobody ever said it's quick.

Not in the slightest.

I started the descent six hours ago. Making a virtue of necessity, I've put the time to good use by reviewing everything I know, not only about laketons in particular but also about the internal structure of eukaryotic cells in general. Just in case.

After all, the giants of Brobdingnag are nothing but hypertrophied eukaryotic cells. I mean, if they were just a zillion times smaller they'd be hard to tell from your average garden-variety amoeba.

Kilometers and kilometers of rigid cable stretching out, *Beagle* descending, and me inside with my database, micronucleus this, macronucleus that, mitochondria here and Golgi apparatus there, and on and on, with the ribosomes and the chloroplasts and the whatnot.

Then the experiment in which Helmut Walpurgis used fifty tons of dye to test for the existence of endoplasmic reticula and sol-gel processes in laketon cytoplasm. And the one by Morph-Khulrry, a brilliant Cetian researcher (credit where credit's due, human or not), who employed radioactive markers to establish the digestive vacuole cycle...

And so many more details, which only convince me of how little we know about Cosita and its species.

I repeat, the major defect of orbital elevators, improvised or not, is that they're much slower than self-propelled vehicles. No such thing as a free lunch. Avoiding acceleration forces means losing time in return for gaining comfort.

In Brobdingnag, with its enormous planetary radius, I face an additional problem: Stationary orbit would put me more than a thousand kilometers above its surface—so the descent would take nearly an entire day, far too long given the urgency of this rescue effort.

I chose instead to be "dropped off" from just 510 kilometers up, an altitude at which there's practically no atmosphere—though you can still feel the tug of gravity, and then some!

As a result, the entire planet is revolving under my *Beagle*.

And if I don't keep my eyes peeled, I might end up dozens of kilometers from Cosita and its prisoners.

This planet is BIG.

Make that IMMENSELY HUGE.

But for now everything's running like clockwork... with a little help from the four laketon observation ships.

The veterinarian biologists (two humans, one Parimazo, two Amphorians, and one Laggoru) now stationed in orbit had to be let in on the operation, whether the secrecy-obsessed military brass liked it or not. Eight of the largest Juhungan ships flying in formation in this sector? And letting down hundreds of kilometers of cable from which a small human-made ship is dangling? No observer could miss that, no matter how sleepy or myopic.

Of course nobody told them I'd be involved. Or who was being rescued.

Quit while you're ahead.

Compartmentalization, they call it.

The military officer hasn't been born who'll willingly reveal anything he can keep under his hat.

Some eleven kilometers above the surface, and fifty-five kilometers north of Cosita, I figure it's time for my *Beagle* to let go of its silk tether and turn from spider into glider.

Crunch time.

That's the message I send to the eight mother ships—but not over the airwaves: secure communications only, over the same cable I'm hanging from. Better not to broadcast the inner workings of this rescue. I'll have to maintain strict radio silence until it's time for me to ask them to let the fishing line down again and get me back into orbit. If everything goes well, not just me but Enti Kmusa and An-Mhaly too, all aboard *Beagle*.

I release the grappling hook and go into free fall for less than a picosecond. Then the on-board computer, which might not be an AI but knows its stuff, finishes calculating the optimal silhouette and wing profile for gliding under six Earth gravities through an atmosphere at least three times as dense.

The result is a very long, needle-nosed fuselage with a delta wing that wouldn't have looked out of place on a supersonic fighter in late twentieth-century Earth.

Not sure if it's more like a Su-27 or an F-15A... I'm no expert in military history.

The missiles complete the picture... I really feel like getting rid of the extra weight by firing them all right now, but better not risk it. I don't even know what kind of explosives they're loaded with. What if the explosions are so powerful they rouse Cosita, or startle it? What if I try to fire them and they blow up in my face?

Of course, no twentieth-century fighter jet would fly this smoothly. But the aerodynamics of a hyperdense atmosphere and high gravity calls for moving as gently as possible. No sudden swerves, no rapid nosedives at sharp angles. Not even all the hydraulic overload-absorption systems I have on board could handle the incredible acceleration caused by abrupt maneuvers.

That's why I just glide down in an almost cowardly way, reducing my velocity kilometer by kilometer with the aerodynamic brakes while overflying the desolate surface of Brobdingnag, dotted here and there with the mobile bluish seas that are its only inhabitants... And right down below me comes Cosita.

Perfect timing, indeed.

Shit. You have no idea how huge it is until you see it close up.

It fills the horizon, even from this altitude. Of course, there's almost two hundred kilometers of it...

Laketons? They could just as well have called them mega-islands. Or minicontinents.

Impressive.

Very, very impressive.

After this inevitable moment of respectful astonishment, I activate my taste-and-smell camouflage. Since laketons have no eyes or ears, the only way for me to trick this one into engulfing me in its digestive vacuole is by pretending to be much tastier than I really am. Play with its senses of smell and taste.

Liquids spray from nozzles located at strategic points along my *Beagle*'s fuselage. A mixture of water and hydrocarbons coat it in a thick soup of substantial nutrients, no doubt in quantities never before witnessed by this enormous extraterrestrial amoeba.

Carbon à la carte. I'm a piece of bait no laketon could pass up—and Cosita doesn't disappoint. I veer smoothly to one side to make sure it's not just waiting to get hit by its food. But no, there's the pseudopod, stretching out to catch me.

I think back to when my mother used to take me to the stadium on Sundays, back in Coaybay. Now the analogy seems more fitting than ever: the laketon looks like a baseball player waiting to catch a pop fly, reaching up with its pseudopod-mitt to trap the ball at all costs.

I've cut my speed to under fifty kilometers an hour. Impact is imminent.

I activate the acceleration-absorption system. Half a ton of soft elastic gel fills every gap between my body and *Beagle's* cockpit. The abrupt reduction in velocity that awaits me won't be fun, but I'll hold up a lot better if I can make myself one with my ship.

*

We haven't received any distress signals from Enti and An. The laketon's bulk might complicate a radio broadcast, but... A terrible suspicion assails me: What if they died, their bones compacted to dust when they hit Cosita, and the most I can hope to accomplish with this whole song and dance is rescue a couple of stiffs?

There'd be such a fuss.

Shit, what an awful thing to occur to me right now...

While I console myself with the thought that the universe can't be such an asshole as to play a nasty trick like that on us after all our plans and preparations, I'm already gliding over the titan.

I bite down on my mouth guard, praying for the worst to be over quickly, and...

Contact!

A perfect catch by center fielder Cosita. A textbook out, and...

...lights out for me.

It was like running head first into a wall. First everything turned red, then black, then I couldn't see at all... until now. Everything hurts, even my spacesuit.

I'm not up to this anymore. I'll never be young again. Time doesn't stand still.

Speaking of time, my first conscious thought is to check and see exactly how much has gone by while I was out of the game. The clock is ticking on this rescue mission, in the form of Cosita's potent digestive enzymes.

Just half an hour. Not too bad. Maybe I'm not so old after all...

The main thing is, I'm inside now. As the instruments confirm.

Others might find sailing through protoplasm gross, but after my recent intestinal adventure in the tsunami it seems like the height of asepsis to me.

Out there, the alimentary vacuole that engulfed me is well on its way to becoming a digestive apparatus. *Beagle* is floating in a sort of translucent broth pullulating with ribosomes and other enchanting cytoplasmic organelles, which are beginning to secrete the necessary acids and enzymes for absorbing my nutritious coating of hydrocarbons and water.

Who'd have thunk. For once, everything's going according to plan. Phase two is working as smoothly as phase one did.

I'm the first veterinarian biologist to penetrate the cellular membrane of a laketon.

Too bad I'm not the first intelligent being, or even the first human being, to do so, and too bad I can't spend weeks here at my leisure, tranquilly observing all the wonders of this unique and colossal organism.

I'm not here for pleasure or to satisfy my scientific curiosity; I have to hurry up and rescue the unfortunate pair who got here before me.

Just a matter of getting out of this vacuole and boldly going through the protoplasm until I find the other digestive vacuole that holds a small Juhungan ship, where Enti and An are trapped. Before Cosita has time to dissolve them, of course.

Simple, isn't it? Much like finding a needle in a haystack two hundred kilometers wide.

How can I reckon my position and direction and set a course when the vehicle I'm driving is surrounded by billions of tons of cytoplasm?

Complicating the situation even more, this protoplasm isn't homogeneous but a colloid with some zones in the high-density solution phase, others in the more aqueous gel phase, all shot through with a sort of internal hive-skeleton: the endoplasmic reticulum. My *Beagle* has magnetohydrodynamic engines to propel it through gel like a submarine through a sea of liquid mercury, but it would get hopelessly mired in the ultradense sol-phase cytoplasm.

I have a few emergency tools to deal with such exigencies, of course... but I'd rather not abuse them. In the process I might throw off Cosita's entire complex metabolic process.

Gardf-Mhaly told me, perhaps to get me excited about the project, that I was embarking on the sort of adventure nineteenth-century boats engaged in when they navigated the Mississippi, a fickle river in earthly North America whose constantly shifting course quickly rendered maps obsolete. The only way ships could keep from running aground in its wide, muddy, treacherous water was to constantly sound its depths—and to count on the almost supernatural skill and intuition of their pilots.

Good metaphor, Gardf. If I make it out of here, I promise to read up on the Mississippi and its heroes.

The only name that comes to mind from that place and time is Mark Twain.

But now it's my turn to imitate... Tom Sawyer? Huck Finn...? using the ship's gyroscopic compass, radar densimeter, and inertial vector gauge, plus my own intuition.

The colossus is moving across the landscape in a north-by-north-northeasterly direction, so I should expect strong gel currents to flow towards what I'll call its "head." The digestive vacuoles, meanwhile, always flow towards the "tail," because, like many living creatures, laketons don't seem especially fond of crawling over their own excrement. So, obviously, if I want to catch up to the vacuole containing Enti and An, I'll have to sail against the current, full speed ahead.

As soon as I get myself out of this vacuole, of course.

First step is to make myself, if not undetectable, at least a little less conspicuous and appetizing.

I apply a weak electrostatic charge to Beagle's fuselage, causing the droplets of petroleum-water emulsion that had made me so succulent to disperse on the spot. Then (three cheers for smart alloys!) I modify the shape of my fuselage to that of a needle-nosed torpedo and aim it straight at the vacuole membrane.

Perfect. Converting speed into penetration force, I cut through the thin barrier like a hot knife through a stick of butter. Some of the vacuole's contents spill out, but a phalanx of organelles is already rushing over to seal the leak. If Cosita were microscopically small and we were on Earth, surface tension would suffice to fix the problem, but gravity on Brobdingnag is six times as powerful and the hole is nearly five meters wide, so an active sealing system is called for.

I leave it all behind; as much as I'd love to observe how the organelles function, I can't dawdle.

I cut my speed to avoid getting mired in a sol-phase zone. Just as I thought: The enormous bubble that is the digestive vacuole I had been sailing through up until a few seconds ago is moving to the back, inside an even larger mass of cytoplasmic gel.

But not much larger. I've traveled a hundred meters at most when the radar densimeter warns me of an upcoming sol-phase zone.

My first barrier reef.

Now I understand why helmsmen and pilots in olden days felt so much respect for people who could navigate or fly by instruments alone, with zero visibility. Trying to navigate a "river" of protoplasm in which you can't tell the "open channels" (gel-phase) from the "shoals" (sol-phase) just by looking at them is equally complicated. Or more so.

All I can see through *Beagle*'s portholes is a uniform blue, through which organelles meander lazily... Some of them, to be sure, have attached themselves to my fuselage, like barnacles to a ship's hull.

They'd better not corrode the alloy, or someone's going to have to zip down and rescue the rescuer.

Time to decide. According to the map I'm getting from the densimeter's low-frequency waves, I've got two options: aim for a weak, narrow current of gel-phase near here, just a hundred meters from where I am now, or opt for a very strong and much broader current (several kilometers wide is my guess) that's almost twice as far off, which means crossing a small but dense region of sol.

I have to choose, quick. The digestive vacuole I broke free from a minute ago is already moving off, and the back end of the gel-phase surrounding and propelling it is coming closer and closer.

Okay, since I'm the Veterinarian to the Giants and I'm inside the biggest giant there is, I head for the big dog and just hope bigger actually is better.

I back up, build up some steam—and here I go, full speed ahead, slamming straight into the sol-phase.

Another out.

Shit and double shit... How could I be so stupid? I completely forgot that, even though I don't feel it so much here inside Cosita, the sextuple gravity operates everywhere on Brobdingnag. The accelerations that come with every collision can cause a lot of damage... Good thing the overload-absorption fluid was automatically discharged when I hit the elastic but tough sol-phase.

Again, it was like running head first into a wall. I was knocked out for nearly ten minutes, and everything hurts now, even more than before. When I get out of here I'll have to get a checkup from an orthopedist... If I even have a skeleton left by then.

I'll also have a psychiatrist check me out, to explain to me why I accepted this mission...

Ironically, according to the densimeter, my massive head-on collision only got me fifteen meters into the sol-phase shoals. Minimal progress, which I then completely squandered while I was unconscious. Everything's moving in here; the large current is now three hundred meters from my current position—not exactly reassuring. I'm completely surrounded by sol-phase, like a fly caught in a cake.

I take a deep breath. Calm down, Jan Amos, analyze the data carefully, there's always at least one way out…

And so there is. I discover that, since every cloud has a silver lining, while I missed my date with the Mississippi, I came a lot closer to its tributary. The weak, narrow current of gel-phase is now less than forty meters from my ship.

This business of navigating through cytoplasm has its ins and outs, I can see.

Too bad we haven't come up with the ideal propulsion system for sailing through thousands of tons of glop the consistency of flan.

I'll have to think this one through. Maybe some kind of screw propeller. For example, mounting giant drills on the prow of *Beagle*…

But since I didn't think of it earlier, for now I'll have to resort to extreme measures.

There's an old Earth proverb: If the mountain won't come to Muhammad, Muhammad must go to the mountain. Even if there aren't many Muslims anymore, it's still a smart attitude.

I'm going to apply it here, with a slight variation: If you're stuck in a medium so dense you can't sail through it—well, then, make it less dense.

I use the nozzles on the sides of *Beagle* to spray a ton and a half of sodium chloride—that is, everyday table salt. And the sol that has me trapped immediately starts liquefying into gel.

I could give myself a standing ovation, but it's just membrane physics: When you abruptly increase the concentration of salts in one zone, osmotic pressure causes an inflow of liquid in order to reestablish an equilibrium.

I move forward exactly twenty-three meters before the protoplasm congeals once more into sol, trapping me in its sticky jaws. I still have to navigate nearly that far again before I'll come out into open gel.

Alright, let's not panic. I've got more salt—enough for at least three more "liquidations" like this. After that, we'll see. If I get stuck again farther on, I'll have to rack my brains...

But I'll cross that bridge when I get to it...

If I get to it, that is.

In the end, there's always brute force.

So here we go again...

Now I push the engines and—a small partial victory that renews my confidence in a great final victory! I manage to emerge into the gel, though by a very narrow margin.

The current carries me away... No, I have to face it, I want to go in the opposite direction. Tough luck. It would have been so easy to let the current take me...

Fortunately, the gel isn't flowing at more than thirty kilometers an hour, and it's only 150 meters wide. It isn't very powerful—whereas my engines are. But even so, it's unspeakably hard for me—first to keep from being swept away, and then to slowly make up for lost ground.

I shudder to think what might have become of me if I had managed to penetrate the other current, the wide, powerful one. I'd be powerless now, swept away by its tremendous force, dragged farther and farther from the people I was supposed to be rescuing, maybe even carried up to Cosita's "head."

I have to be better at thinking things through—preferably before acting. Up to now I've been navigating (literally) by good luck, but fortune won't smile on me forever.

As if to make up for these moments of stress, the next hour and a half is fairly monotonous.

I even allow myself a couple of quick naps, which do wonders for calming my nerves and giving my tortured body some rest.

Autopilot takes over the steering on *Beagle*... and each time we approach a fork in the gel river, the radar densimeter alarm gives me nearly a one-minute warning so I can choose which way to go.

To pretend I know where I'm going and lend an appearance of method to what is nothing but a random search, I always pick the right fork. Standard method in any labyrinth.

Laggoru magnetohydrodynamic propulsion, much more efficient than propellers and now used for powering aquatic vehicles by all the "lucky seven" races, allows a ship to travel several hundred kilometers an hour—under one Earth gravity.

But under six gravities, and completely immersed in a medium much denser than water, a speed of seventy kilometers an hour is more than acceptable.

Since I wasn't foresighted enough to stow a bubble generator on board *Beagle* for dealing with laminar-turbulent-flow
interface problems, this is the fastest I can go in this cytoplasm
without running into cavitation trouble...

Roughly seventy kilometers an hour, but from that I have
to subtract the thirty kilometers an hour that the gel current's
moving. Curiously, the gel continues to flow at a steady rate even
as I steer into narrower and narrower branches. What would
Bernoulli say? Forty kilometers an hour, net, and I still don't
know where I'm going.

But I'm an optimist. I unequivocally expect to arrive some-
where or other before this bug's powerful enzymes digest the
Juhungan bioship with my two former employees inside it.

Or at least before the eighth intelligent race with the technological capability for faster-than-light travel appears in the
galaxy...

And just when I'm giving in to these melancholic reflections,
the magnetometer alarm rings.

I'd love to shout, "Eureka!" But I control myself, because I'm
no Archimedes.

Who said it was impossible? I've found the needle in the
haystack.

Or at least I have a rough idea of where in the haystack
it is.

Because localizing a few dozen kilos of metal, which is to say,
all the magnetic material contained in the Juhungan bioship

where Enti Kmusa and An-Mhaly are trapped, is still very different from being able to get there.

According to this ultrasensitive instrument, the girls and their ship are barely three hundred meters from here—but they might as well be in another galaxy. Between me and them lies nothing but sol-phase cytoplasm. And I've already learned how hard it is to force my way through that living flan.

For a second, despair overcomes me; I'm still drawing closer, and less than half a minute from now I'll be as close as I can get to where they are, after which I'll start moving away...

With them so close, could I really resign myself to not being able to...?

No way.

I'm not moving from this spot, to start with.

I deploy an anchor, a sort of metal claw on one end of a cable, which shoots out and sinks deep into the sol. It'll stop me from moving till I can figure out how to get to Enti and An, who are now barely a hundred fifty meters from me...

Till I think of something...

It's unfair. Have I swum so far just to drown here by the shore? Why won't some brilliant idea pop into my head right now? Why can't I be a holoseries hero, like the ones that always killed me even though they were so much smaller and weaker than me when I played giants on Anima Mundi? One of those characters who grow when the going gets tough?

I can't crash into the sol protoplasm barrier using *Beagle* as a battering ram. I'd hardly get anywhere, and the crash alone could break my neck. If it isn't broken already, I mean.

And I don't have enough salt left to liquefy this much sol-phase cytoplasm by osmosis. There's hundreds, maybe thousands of tons of the stuff.

I look desperately at the distance gauge; it's showing 156 meters now... and growing.

Shit. I'm fuming. It's enough to make you pull out a pistol and shoot yourself.

If I only had one...

Wait a sec!

That's it!

A pistol.

I do have a pistol, and it's a HUGE one.

Of course I didn't bring any personal weapons aboard, whether sonic, projectile, or laser. What could I have done with one? Shoot Cosita? Blow out my brains before I died of asphyxiation or hunger if I got trapped in its cytoplasm?

We veterinarian biologists rarely fire anything but anesthetizing dart guns. Though, given my specialty, I've sometimes been tempted to use anesthetizing cannons.

But as it happens, *Beagle* is all one enormous gun—and I suspect it's well loaded.

Who knows, but I won't end up thanking that stuck-up Kurchatov for his intransigent militarism. And I'll owe him one, precisely for not allowing me to remove the missiles from the magazines.

I just hope I'm able to fire them.

Let's see...

On-board computer, what munitions am I carrying?

DATA UNAVAILABLE. TO UNLOCK OPERATIVE CAPA-BILITIES OF ON-BOARD WEAPON SYSTEMS, PLEASE INPUT PERSONAL PASSWORD OF GENERAL JUNICHIRO KURCHATOV. AWAITING INPUT.

Shit and triple shit. I'm sitting inside a gun loaded with God knows what, I don't know where the safety is... and the computer has automatically defaulted to "don't touch me unless you're an officer" mode, blocking me from pulling the trigger.

Twelve characters? It could be anything... But I have to try. Try thinking like them. Kurchatov. Military. He once told me that Igor Kurchatov was the father of the Russian atomic bomb. Fix it up a little, and maybe...

Atomicbomber.

PASSWORD NOT RECOGNIZED.

No, it's not going to be easy, like in a holoseries. But, twelve characters?

What if I misjudged him? What if all the disdain I thought he was showing for me was just envy and nostalgia for the good old times we had as students partying at Anima Mundi?

Let's see, I'll try it. If it's a reference to veterinarian biology, what password would my old party buddy Juni Tacho pick? Ecology? Evolution? Seven and nine letters, too short. Cellularbiology? Fifteen, too long. What about my name? How ironic would that be... JanAmosSangan... No, could have worked, but it's thirteen characters. Some professor, maybe—Argol Swendal? With no space it's twelve letters. But forget it, Kurchatov hated symbolic logic, had a tutor assigned to help him both semesters. Raul Pineda? No, we only had classes with him in the fifth year, so Tacho never met him, and his name only has eleven characters even with the space. Besides, Juni Tacho didn't bother going to classes very often; he was too busy hanging out in bars, cantinas, and other dives...

Heh.

Bars, cantinas, and dives. Could be. And it has exactly twelve letters.

But it's so unserious. Well, it's not like we were all that serious at Anima Mundi.

Besides, I imagine I'll get three chances to guess the password.

I'm sure this can't be right, either. In the holoseries, the hero always guesses it on the final attempt.

But before I get to my third try, I have to do my second.

Oceanography.

PASSWORD ACCEPTED. WELCOME ABOARD, GENERAL KURCHATOV. ITEMIZING MUNITIONS CAPABILITIES: 46 MISSILES. 8 THERMONUCLEAR

WARHEADS (20 KILOTONS EACH). 16 THERMOBARIC WARHEADS. 22 DIRECTIONAL HIGH-IMPACT BUNKER BUSTERS. ALL READY FOR USE. DO YOU WISH TO LOAD ANY?

A gun? Nope: *Beagle* is a fucking arsenal. I can't believe it. Eight thermonuclear warheads? 160 kilotons? They weren't just planning to get rid of me and Enti and An if things went downhill... I doubt even Cosita would survive an explosion of that magnitude going off inside its guts. They could have blown a hole in the planet Brobdingnag itself. How ridiculous.

Military brass. Always ready to blow everything up, obsessed with the power of destruction. It must have driven them crazy to find creatures like laketons in the galaxy that would just laugh at all their weaponry!

Naturally, sooner or later they'd want to prove who's who.

But now it's me with my finger on the trigger. Twenty-two "directional high-impact bunker busters"? Let's see if they can open a path for me through... exactly 159 meters of sol-phase cytoplasm.

Shamelessly impersonating Kurchatov, I set the target coordinates, order the missile launch, and there goes the first one... And I'm still acting as thoughtlessly as before. Will the missile even work in liquid?

Turns out it does. It uses gas jets for propulsion, sending it off amazingly fast. Now I just need an explosion.

BOOOOOM.

It's made a hole almost ten meters deep. I launch the second. BOOOOOM. And the third. BOOOOOM. What if I launch two at once? BOOOOOMBOOOOOM...

They don't make quite as spectacular an explosion when they go off together; better space them out a little bit.

BOOOOOM   BOOOOOM   BOOOOOM   BOOOOOM BOOOOOM...

Seventeen missiles later, whoever said that brute force never solved anything? Handled properly, it can perform miracles.

I suppose I'll have to explain how I guessed General Kurchatov's secret password to the gatekeepers from Military Security, and also answer for each of the missiles I just fired as if they were members of my own family.

I hope they cost less than my reward for rescuing the girls. Otherwise, I might be in serious trouble; the military doesn't like it when folks mess around with their toys, much less their budgets.

But the main thing is that now I've blasted a way clear through for my *Beagle*.

I drive on, a little worried to find my path closing up this fast behind me.

Aftershocks rumble through the protoplasm. Maybe the explosions were directional, but Cosita must be asking itself what's going on. I don't think it comes down with digestive ailments very often.

But over there, at last, I see the digestive vacuole where my old assistants are trapped. One last little push with all engines blasting, and I punch through the membrane...

Well, that wasn't so hard, after all.

I'm inside now.

Shit, what if I didn't get here in time...

Cosita's digestive enzymes are stronger than we thought. Or else laketons find the carbon-reinforced germanium foam in Juhungan bioships more tempting than we'd figured.

I can barely recognize the ship's original form, it's so deteriorated. Whole chunks are gone. The outer shell isn't a shadow of its former self. And forget about it being hermetically sealed.

I gulp. Did Enti and An manage to...?

They did; there they are, alive and kicking. They must have detected me the moment I blasted my way through. They waddle over in their ultraprotective suits, which fortunately aren't organic. The suits are too heavy to swim in, as I should have expected. At least they can still walk, leaning against the vacuole membrane for support.

I open the airlock—and they're inside. A quick decontamination cycle, off with the suits, which are a little deteriorated after all—this vacuole is pure acid—and then...

I'm no fan of gratuitous pathos, so I won't linger over a description of the scene that comes next: how they crawl and drag themselves into the cabin, how they hug me (An-Mhaly rubs her six pectoral protuberances all over me, and I don't object), how they kiss me, cry, accuse each other, accuse their bosses, their subordinates, Cosita, the Galactic Community Coordinating Committee, and the universe itself.

The important thing is, they're both unharmed, though pretty shaken up.

But no time for gushing; we've got to get out of here.

This second.

First, out of the vacuole—because even *Beagle*'s theoretically inert metal casing is under attack from the aggressive enzymes, and suffering for it. And it's made from a smart alloy that can't regenerate at all, unlike living tissue, unfortunately.

A short engine pulse—and we're out.

The bad thing is that now, according to the radar densimeter, there aren't any gel-phase currents within several kilometers of here.

Am I going to have to use more missiles? I never found brute force very convincing as a solution to all my problems. Besides, it would take too many...

I explain things to my two new passengers, since they always say three heads are better than one... and An-Mhaly comes up with the idea that might save us: Why worry about extracting yourself from a place when it's easy enough to get yourself kicked out?

All we have to do is make ourselves so undesirable and uncomfortable that Cosita expels us of its own accord.

Seconds later, I discharge all the salt I have left, together with two tons of colchicine (an eighty-percent concentration), into the cytoplasm around *Beagle.*

I knew it would come in handy.

It's like pouring gasoline onto an anthill and setting it afire.

Cosita writhes in pain. But can this giant really feel pain?

Then, in less time than it takes to tell the story, we're encased in an excretory vacuole, and three minutes later we're expelled.

Hurray for the instinct of self-preservation.

Free at last!

It was practically child's play.

The rest of the rescue, including our return to orbit via the nanotube cables suspended from the Juhungan ships, is mere routine, little more than retracing my steps. Though to lift us in this gravity, the heroic *Beagle* has to give every remaining drop of its strength.

I had to believe, but from the time Gardf-Mhaly first contacted me to the moment she and her milk cousin embraced (back to back, as is their people's bizarre custom), only sixteen hours have passed.

And just thirty-two hours passed from the moment the human and the Cetian fell into Cosita's alimentary vacuole to when they were freed.

I dare anybody to do it better—or faster.

*

All's well that ends well, as somebody once said.

Enti Kmusa and An-Mhaly returned home, unharmed and on time, and no one guessed why they had taken so long or what they'd been up to in the meantime. The super-duper-top-secret negotiations between Cetians and Olduvailans remained under wraps.

The human, Cetian, and Juhungan generals and Coordinators breathed a sigh of relief.

And, as they had all hoped, after the two negotiators reached a fair (and ultraconfidential) solution to the New Olduvai/Canaan/ Urgh-Yhaly-Mhan disagreement, hostilities ceased.

The fifty-five thousand illegal colonizers remaining on Canaan, feeling undefeated, agreed to relocate to the second planet of Theta Muscae. Not as green or as fertile as New Olduvaila, but at least nobody else had ever claimed it before.

They named it Mvambaland. And who did they unanimously elect president but Enti Kmusa. That didn't even take me by surprise.

The Cetians finally occupied Urgh-Yhaly-Mhan. Their Assimilation master was An-Mhaly, whose chief adviser was her milk cousin, Coordinator Gardf.

General Junichiro Kurchatov tried to lecture me about my unauthorized use of the missiles, but since nobody asks a winner for receipts... Let's just say, they took the cost of the seventeen bunker-buster missiles out of what they paid me for "valuable services rendered."

Which added up to quite a discount, but still, twelve million solaria ("we threw un pequeño incentivo for you to mantenerlo todo hush-hush," said Admiral William Hurtado) is enough money that I wasn't going to start complaining about a minor though fundamentally unfair tax.

On the other hand, good thing I didn't use the thermonuclear warheads or I'd still be paying for them.

Truth is, I wasn't expecting medals or public recognition (a secret's a secret), but what I liked least about the whole deal was not being able to talk about it with anyone.

Not with my parents, who, for their part, each kept on grumbling that I'd wasted my life mucking through slime and mucilage.

Not with the eight veterinarian biologists from different species who had "observed" the whole rescue mission from their four observation vessels orbiting Brobdingnag.

Not even with Narbuk. To my endless surprise, and I suspect also to the amazement of the ecologists on Abyssalia, my secretary-assistant had dealt with the out-of-season spawning of the grendels with consummate skill. And entirely on his own! Though he never came within two kilometers of any of the gigantic crustaceans, it took him no more than twenty-six hours to analyze the water and discover the biochemical pollutant that, even in extremely diluted concentrations, was disrupting the critters' life cycle.

How smug he was when he told me!

If he only knew...

As a reward for his splendid independent performance, I prepared a dish of fried eggplant with seasoned tomatoes and capers. And he loved it.

After wolfing down his second helping, the impudent little fellow hinted he'd like to set himself up on his own as a second "Veterinarian to the Giants."

Fine by me, I told him. A little competition lends spice to life.

But he shouldn't even dream of me lending him the money to get his business started.

And the slogan was all my idea.

Fair's fair, but too much is too much. Love your neighbor as yourself, sure—but not more than yourself.

And Cosita?

Fine, thanks. From what we could tell, it hadn't even noticed anything.

And that's where matters would have ended, with no further repercussions, all of us more or less satisfied. Except my parents, of course. And grumpy old Juni Tacho, maybe.

But the fact is, the story didn't end there.

Not at all.

Three weeks after my lucky rescue, the veterinarian biologists orbiting Brobdingnag (new ones, of course, not the same eight) noticed that Cosita was starting to display behaviors no one had ever seen in a laketon.

First it stopped moving, regardless of how many tasty cometoids rich in carbonaceous chondrites fell within a few hundred meters of it. It didn't even stir when other, smaller laketons ate them, taking advantage of its peculiar quiescence.

It didn't react to anything.

Over the following weeks, its enormous body began to reorganize as it slowly took the shape of a giant cone whose apex towered nearly thirty-five kilometers above the ground. A living mountain that left even the famous Olympus Mons of Mars in the dust.

Its cytoplasm also changed from a translucent blue to pitch black, and its cell wall seemed to grow markedly harder, until it assumed nearly the consistency of horn.

Since it gave no signs of metabolic activity, the general opinion was that Cosita was dying... and everyone was getting ready to observe that exceptional event.

It would be sort of like witnessing the death of a god.

When I found out, I admit I felt pretty guilty. Could I have killed it, what with the missiles, and the salt, and the colchicine?

Half the galaxy was fixated on Brobdingnag for the next two weeks. Until one fine day, after some people had started to think nothing else would happen, when suddenly Cosita exploded.

Not a metaphor.

It literally EXPLODED.

A good part of the matter that formed it was ejected at high speed from the small "crater" that opened up at the apex.

The living mountain really was a volcano, it turns out. Except that when it erupted, instead of red-hot lava, in a final titanic effort it ejected billions upon billions of oval capsules, barely half a meter across each.

Spores!

Due to the tremendous gravity on Brobdingnag, almost ninety percent of that eruption of life fell right back onto the planet's surface, though some of them landed thousands of kilometers away.

I'm certain that some of them will germinate.

But the lucky and determined ten percent of these condensed seeds of life did escape into space, where they dispersed in every direction.

And that's when the trouble started all over again.

My colleagues were thrilled. They'd finally solved the long-standing mystery of how laketons reproduce! And it was as spectacular as everything else having to do with the titans of Brobdingnag!

So many fascinating new questions now arose. Could those traveling spores be the original panspermia that had dispersed from the depths of the cosmos and gave rise to oxygen-based life on so many worlds in the galaxy? (Oh, Arrhenius, what you're missing!) Could we Laggorus, humans, and Cetians all be distant descendants of Cosita, Tiny, and company? Since all three species share DNA as our means of transmitting and replicating biological information, that could well be the case...

More research was called for. And since inorganic machines hold up better to extreme accelerations than their makers, a variety of automatic probes were soon on their way to the surface of Brobdingnag to recover some of the millions of spores that hadn't made it off the planet.

That's when they discovered something very curious.

As is usually the case with spores, each contained all the genetic information needed to give rise to a new laketon, an exact replica of Cosita.

Or rather, not quite exact... Because, buried inside the DNA, there were a few curious chains that had hydrogen and germanium foam bases. What the...? The three or four distinguished Juhungan biologists on the team immediately identified these chains as coming from one of their bioships.

One of the biologists even broached the possibility that, merely by physically penetrating the laketon without exchanging genetic material with it, a Juhungan vehicle could have set its reproductive mechanism in motion.

Unheard of. A Juhungan bioship had fertilized Cosita? But how? Why? And when?

I could have explained the whole thing to them. Apparently, the final dose of salt and colchicine I administered to Cosita to force it to release us must have sent its metabolism into crisis mode, and its nucleus must have decided that under such harsh conditions the best thing to do was sporulate.

But the weirdest and most awful thing was that since the remains of the Juhungan bioship were still inside the digestive vacuole at the time, its genetic information must have gotten mixed up with Cosita's. So the bioship's genes were reproduced billions of times, in each and every one of the spores.

An original... plus n tending to infinity copies.

Even at this point, properly managed, there wouldn't have been any scandal.

But of course, given the military's secrecy complex, it didn't occur to any of them to warn the Juhungans not to analyze the elements of their bioship they found inserted in the laketon genetic code carried by the spores.

Likewise, no one had let Enti Kmusa or An-Mhaly know that the biocomputers built (or cultivated, actually) by the deaf and blind hydrogen breathers function as virtual black boxes, preserving a full record of every operation they carry out.

Since the representatives of the two opposing camps had nothing else to do while captive in the cytoplasm, they'd used their ship's on-board computer to finalize the details of the Olduvailan-Cetian treaty. It turns out, all the details of their top-secret negotiations were recorded inside every one of Cosita's spores.

And millions of them were now zooming all over the galaxy, no less.

We should acknowledge that the Juhungan biologists behaved properly: as soon as they discovered what had happened, they immediately reported it to their bosses, who were already up to speed on the whole affair.

But by then it was too late to stop the avalanche. Veterinarian biologists were flocking to Brobdingnag to investigate Cosita's sporulation, and it had occurred to plenty of them that there was something strange about finding Juhungan bioship records encoded in the spores... So they set about deciphering the DNA, no easy task. That's how they learned about the secret treaty between Olduvaila and Tau Ceti. And all the rest.

In less than three hours, every ship that found a spore in space, every planet where a spore was found orbiting—the whole galaxy, in a word, would learn about the supersensitive accord.

It was a disaster.

A genuine credibility crisis for the Galactic Community Coordinating Committee.

The Amphorians, Laggorus, Kerkants, even the Parimazos, all burst into laughter, not so much at our human and Cetian obsession for keeping up appearances as at our obvious inability to do so successfully.

The Juhungans, with their lame excuses, just added fuel to the fire.

Feeling they had been made fools of in front of the whole galaxy, the former Olduvailans, now Mvambese, rose up in arms against their leaders, demanding instant death for those who had shamed them.

The brand-new planet's entire governing cabinet was tried, found guilty... and executed.

Luckily for President Enti, she wasn't on her planet at the time; that was the only reason she escaped her fellow citizens' fury.

They've also demanded my head, by the way, but a planet's sentences are only valid on its surface... Well, there are still lots of other worlds in the Milky Way for me to visit, aren't there? And Mvambaland isn't high on my list.

The Cetians, as dramatic as the Olduvailan-Mvambese, though I admit rather less bloodthirsty, passed an irrevocable sentence on the Assimilation master in their new colony on Urgh-Yhaly-Mhan, my old secretary-assistant An-Mhaly: banishment from their culture for life. And the hunt for scapegoats to answer for the "affront to the honor of the Goddess's own People" did not stop there. An-Mhaly's milk cousin, Gardf, lost her position on the Galactic Community Coordinating Committee, and along with Conflictmaster Jhun-Likha was condemned to "ritual death": returning to the same Cetian sea from which they had once emerged as shivering eel-like spawn, entering it dressed in the full garb and regalia of their offices, and emerging without insignia or clothes, and with new names.

But still alive, at least.

I pity them for their political ambitions. I really do. I had come to feel... a kind of affection for them. And their downfall doesn't make me happy.

Actually, given that they both had enough inner strength not to commit suicide when their reputations were ruined, I'm fairly confident they'll win back prestige and responsibility. Though it may take some time.

As for me, the agent of their race's discredit, I was forbidden to set foot ever again in any Cetian colony or ship anywhere in the galaxy, under penalty of death. And all the lovely six-breasted humanoids were informed that it was taboo to even think of contacting me.

That really did hurt. Cetians used to be my best clients.

Admiral Hurtado and General Kurchatov were likewise immediately demoted. I think Juni Tacho went back to Anima Mundi to resume his studies of veterinarian biology, but I haven't confirmed it.

I suspect he's really trying with all his might to get a PhD in oceanography. Bar to bar, dive to dive...

The Army and Space Force of Earth tried to sue me over my "unauthorized utilization of classified military materiel," based on the episode of the seventeen bunker busters, and they demanded I return the "material incentive received for disinterested assistance" to pay for "moral damages"...

But I'm not Enti or An. I stopped them dead in their tracks; if they kept pressing their ridiculous claim, I'd divulge every detail about the ultrasecret design of *Beagle*...

They gulped and dropped the matter.

In fact—in order to save face, I suppose—they actually gave me a medal.

We'll consider ourselves even, then.

Though if I look at the whole balance sheet, I came out ahead. Pretty far ahead.

My parents aren't ashamed of me anymore; they proudly tell everyone they're the parents of the famous "Veterinarian to the Giants." My client list, though now deprived of six-breasted Cetians seeking my services, is almost twice as long as before. The Brobdingnag incident was great publicity for me. It sure didn't hurt when that rascal Narbuk updated my holonet site with images of my daring rescue of the victims trapped inside the second largest laketon in the universe.

Don't ask me how he got the pictures... I actually think most of them are fakes.

Life goes on.

I recently heard that the Governor Tarkon was unexpectedly deposed on Nerea. A scandal involving the illegal trafficking of (why am I not surprised?) tsunami fecal pearls. With the Amphorians.

His whereabouts are currently unknown. And will remain so for quite a while, I expect. He faces corruption charges that could keep him behind bars for the rest of his life.

They say his worthy spouse has disowned him and is now in a torrid relationship with one of her former bodyguards. That's the latest scandal on the Nerean holonews. Seems it's the same guard who harpooned the tsunami so skillfully with the radio tag that allowed me to identify the bracelet eater.

To think there are still people who say women are ungrateful.

I don't bear the lady any ill will. After all, you only live once. But I hope, for her own good, she isn't dumb enough to give her damned Aldebaran topaz-inlaid platinum wedding bracelet to her muscular new love interest—assuming Tarkon let her keep it, of course.

By the way, I've changed my advertising slogan. Now the sign on my office door simply says:

SUPER EXTRA GRANDE

IF IT'S ONLY MEDIUM-SIZED, DON'T EVEN BOTHER

I can barely keep up with all the clients demanding my services. That's why I'm not worried about the Laggoru's threats to start his own business. The waiting list for my service calls is months long, in spite of all the juggling my three secretary-assistants do to streamline things.

That's right, three. For now, I've still got Narbuk-Alr-Quamal-Tahlir-Norgai on my payroll. After his distinguished service on Abyssalia, it's the least he deserves. Though he constantly reminds me that he wants to fly solo. One of these days.

But he still hasn't done it. For the record.

Oh—and I found out he's not exactly a member of the male sex. A week ago, without really bothering to explain it to me at all, he gave me notice he'd be having cubs in a few months.

After he's had them and they've grown big enough, I guess he'll leave me. We'll figure things out at that point.

As for my two other assistants...

Could I really have slammed the door in the faces of Enti and An, when neither of them had anywhere else to go?

I'm not stonyhearted. Not in the least. So, considering how prosperous I've become, I called them back to my side.

I've made so much money lately, in fact, that I even allowed myself the luxury of acquiring a hissing dragon of Siddhartha. It's still a little thing, barely twenty-five meters long, which is why I'm sure I'll be able to domesticate it before it reaches full size. It already recognizes me and everything. Every time it sees me come in, it excretes especially thick clouds of sulfurous vapor. Lovely.

Concholants are still missing from my résumé, but maybe one of these days I'll have the tremendous pleasure of flying off into space to visit one, even if I don't get paid for it. At least I now have the ideal vehicle for making the trip: I just bought a surplus ship off the Juhungans. It's a twin of the one Enti and An were flying when the laketon captured them.

Don't even ask how much it cost me. Those hydrogen breathers are a bunch of incorrigible skinflints.

Of course, it isn't the same ship, and it isn't *Beagle*, but it serves my needs perfectly, in addition to motivating me and reminding me of the strange case that changed my life.

Until I have an adequate hangar built, it also serves as a den for my two dozen cuddly marbusses from Mizar. I've got it parked in the backyard of the house I share with Enti Kmusa and An-Mhaly...

Yes, I'm living in a peculiar relationship... with both ladies. Hence the marbusses. They really do love them. All women do. And since I love making them happy...

Long live threesomes, if they bring happiness. And the hell with all my prudish old intolerant ideas about exotic women, together with my equally misogynistic prejudices towards non-*Homo sapiens* females, humanoids or gynecoids, with yellow pupil-less eyes, cephalic crests, violet skin, six breasts, three-forked tongues, cartilaginous chewing plates—and oral sex as the main dish on their limited but sincere erotic menu.

Maybe it's my professional success, but now we're the main topic of gossip on all the holonews programs out of Gea. There's also the fact that none of us is exactly tiny, so we three are hard to miss when we're out walking around town, hand in hand.

But I don't care. Let them talk, if that's what they want.

We don't care.

Now I can say I've tried everything.

And to my own surprise, I've discovered that sometimes different is synonymous with interesting.

That getting along and living in harmony takes more than tolerating difference. You have to go a little bit farther, you have to enjoy the diversity.

Polymorphous perverts? Lustful, lewd bisexuals? Sinners destined for the eternal fires of hell?

Bah. Could be. Except for the hell part, that is.

And so what?

It's delightful.

Besides, are we hurting anybody, somehow?

Aren't we adults, all three?

Why do people always try to force pleasure into such strictly human pigeonholes? Sin, propriety, perversity... Humph.

After all, strictly speaking, my "black panther" and I are the only actual couple in this ménage à trois. An, our common platonic partner (though sometimes a bit more than platonic, to tell the truth), is at most a "friend with touching privileges" for both of us, right?

Of course, the touching is oral... And, yes, they were right; it really is exquisite. For the record.

SEPTEMBER 15, 2009

ABOUT THE AUTHOR

Born José Miguel Sánchez Gómez, YOSS assumed his pen name in 1988, when he won the Premio David in the science-fiction category for *Timshel*. Together with his peculiar pseudonym, the author's aesthetic of an impenitent rocker has allowed him to stand out among his fellow Cuban writers. Earning a degree in Biology in 1991, he went on to graduate from the first ever course on Narrative Techniques at the Onelio Jorge Cardoso Center of Literary Training, in 1999. Today, Yoss writes both realistic and science-fiction works. Alongside these novels, the author produces essays, reviews, and compilations, and actively promotes the Cuban science-fiction literary workshops Espiral and Espacio Abierto.

ABOUT THE TRANSLATOR

When he isn't translating, DAVID FRYE teaches Latin American culture and society at the University of Michigan. Translations include *The First New Chronicle and Good Government* by Felipe Guaman Poma de Ayala (Peru, 1615); *The Mangy Parrot* by José Joaquín Fernández de Lizardi (Mexico, 1816), for which he received a National Endowment for the Arts Fellowship; *Writing across Cultures: Narrative Transculturation in Latin America* by Ángel Rama (Uruguay, 1982); and several Cuban and Spanish novels and poems.

RESTLESS BOOKS is an independent publisher for readers and writers in search of new destinations, experiences, and perspectives. From Asia to the Americas, from Tehran to Tel Aviv, we deliver stories of discovery, adventure, dislocation, and transformation.

Our readers are passionate about other cultures and other languages. Restless is committed to bringing out the best of international literature—fiction, journalism, memoirs, poetry, travel writing, illustrated books, and more—that reflects the restlessness of our multiform lives.

Visit us at www.restlessbooks.com.